Untaken: 12 Hours Following the Rapture

C.O. Wyler

Published by C.O. Wyler, 2022.

This is a work of fiction. Similarities to real people, places, or events are entirely coincidental.

UNTAKEN: 12 HOURS FOLLOWING THE RAPTURE

First edition. February 13, 2022.

ISBN: 979-8201886240

Written by C.O. Wyler.

To Lois ~ Thank you for your support, love, prayers, and friendship.

~ Woman ~

My brother. Leave it to him to pull something like this at the last minute. I know he means well, but must he always put me in an awkward position? He may be years older than I am, but he needs to stop bossing me around and constantly pushing my buttons. He's been doing it for decades, as long as I've been alive. But what can I do? I'm a woman in my fifties and have been around the block long enough to know what I like or don't like. Thanks for the gift; it was thoughtful, but why would I want to read this book? *Untaken*? Yeah, "untaken" from what? And why does it involve only twelve hours? Believe me, I won't be taken in again by him.

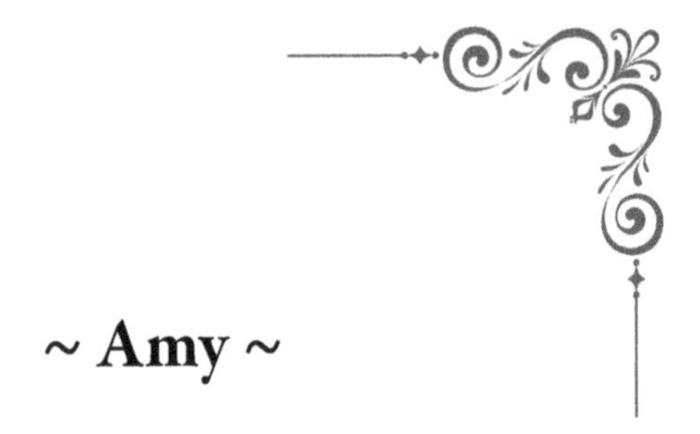

~ Amy ~

Hi. Welcome to my world.

Guess you're here in my mind, in my life, and (I hope) not in my way. I didn't ask you to be here with me witnessing this blow-by-blow account of my current life; you've come here of your own free will, by your choice. I certainly didn't twist your arm; remember that, and remember you can leave whenever you want. You're the one in control of how often you access my thoughts.

I get it—it's the way the world is now with artificial intelligence. Thanks to the Internet of Things, electronic units read your mind while listening to every conversation in your house, car, or workplace. Within seconds, social media barrages you with ads for hot tubs if you clicked on any website that mentioned them. If you're in an auto accident, your smartphone determines your exact location and sends first responders to you before you reach out to them. When the milk in your refrigerator expires, it can be reordered without your having to make the request. City cameras monitor your every move, including when you make a left turn on a yellow light. Via high-resolution satellites, the government can see how many people are in your bedroom doing who knows what.

And now, people can get into your brain and read your thoughts.

Forgive me. I'm not quite used to the idea of having this complex AI neural network accessing my mind. It may be convenient for shopping and flipping through television channels or inputting photo captions for work, of course, all without speaking aloud or lifting a finger, but can you really hear my thoughts? See what I'm seeing on your computer or smartphone screen? And, most astonishing, why would you subscribe to *my* thought-streaming? I'm not even famous yet, but here you are, aware of everything I do, say, or think.

Please don't misunderstand me or think I don't want you here. You're in my head, watching every move I make, every blink I take, observing it all through my eyes while considering my opinions and perspective. I didn't design the program that way; it is a preliminary experiment that I'm getting paid to do. Like I'm always telling my husband, we need to work together and figure things out; we need to be a team. Isn't that the current slogan of the decade, "Help others" or "Pass it forward"? You're here to help me—you're a team player, right? So, let's do this.

Since you entered my life this second, you know virtually nothing about me nor I about you. You'll learn soon enough about my personality, attitude, values, beliefs, and more. Don't judge me, as I have no way of reciprocating. I can't be familiar with you. I have no way of being your friend unless we somehow become connected on social media or meet for coffee or a drink. There's a chance I may be a Type A person and you a Type B, one of us in control, always in the know, and the other more relaxed and easy-going. That's fine, but understand we are different individuals with different memories, motives, and experiences. You may relate and get me, or you may think I'm self-absorbed, nitpicky, and frigid. Fine. I could say good or bad things about you, too, if I were in your head.

It's like what I would expect of you if you were my caddy during a round of golf: I'd tell you to "show up, keep up, and shut up." Well, that does seem a bit harsh, especially when you get to know me, but time will tell.

So hang in there, and things will make sense soon, even if you think you're more confused than I am.

Now, I'll get back to the ranting I was doing before you arrived, and since you're here now, I'll rhetorically ask your advice: What would you do?

I'll explain it simply: I hate her; I hate her. Hear me: I. Hate. Her. And I think you would, too.

The audacity of that woman butting into my life, our lives. How dare she! Who does she think she is? Can't she realize that I'm not her and never want to be her? I bet you wouldn't want to be her, either. Ugh, I hate her. She doesn't get it. Leave me alone; leave us alone!

You watch my hand reach up and grab my straight, long, naturally blonde hair hanging down one side of my face as I tuck a section of it behind my ear, considering whether I should cut it short again. Denny likes it cropped above the shoulders, neat and trim, but I prefer it carefree, wild, and blowing in the wind when I drive around in my bright-yellow VW convertible, top down, in the Southern California sun.

I roll up the sleeves of my thin white shirt and head for the kitchen sink. Tonight's dirty dishes are screaming for attention.

I fill the basin with hot, sudsy water and plunge the encrusted lasagna pan into it to soak.

It's a little awkward for me, knowing you're here in my head. I try to silence my thoughts by concentrating on the counter, black specks embedded in tan granite. But I'm too steamed to focus on them.

Forcing my brain to ignore what has been constantly bothering me all day, I redirect my thinking to something positive. I love our townhouse. We bought the eighteen-hundred-square-foot two-story fourteen months ago while the prices were starting to go up once again in Granada Hills, a suburb of Los Angeles, known to us natives as "the Valley." I'm happy here. Yes, we have traffic, crime, gangs, and every ethnic restaurant possible within walking distance from each other, but this is where I grew up. This is my town, my city. I'm a true Valley girl and proud of it, despite its crowds, rude people, and helicopters frequently circling in the middle of the night, their bright lights searching for the bad guys.

Do you love or enjoy where you are in life? Most of the time I'm happy. But not today.

My husband and I love this condo. When I showed Denny pictures of it online, we both knew it would be perfect the minute we saw its layout: a spacious great room/kitchen/dining area with three bedrooms and two full baths upstairs. Best of all, it's a corner unit with only one wall abutting the neighbors. I concede that it was overpriced, but isn't any property in LA County these days?

Back to my tirade, which I'm sure you want to know more about; I won't leave you hanging. I'll scrub the death out of this pan if I get all huffy over someone like her. It isn't right.

Ah, my husband's aunt. The ever-present, ever-nagging, ever-everything you'd expect of the nosy, busybody, pushy, never-married aunt, Ms. Amy Colton.

I felt it the day I met her. Denny warned me. Yes, he explained her overbearing nature in his considerate, thoughtful manner. His aunt has been and will always be a control freak and must have everything her way. He told me stories of how she bases every decision on whether it's right or wrong, good or evil, or punishment instead of reward. Always repercussions and consequences. No fun, no silliness, no joking around, no nothing. A boring life, a dull upbringing, and—always—a following-the-letter-of-the-law attitude. Do you know that kind of person? I'm sure you have one in your life, too. A parent maybe? A spouse? Friend or coworker? Everybody does.

Tragically, when Denny was ten years old and his brother, Hal, was eight, their parents died in a car accident on curvy Mulholland Drive, and Amy had to deal with raising her brother's sons. Single, with no parenting experience, she made sure the two were properly raised in every conceivable way. In all fairness, I wouldn't have wanted to be in her shoes; it would be hard to raise two boys at any age. I should give her kudos for trying, even if she botched it in several aspects. In my book, parenting is no fun.

Denny's dad shouldn't have been on one of his drinking binges on Christmas Eve when he drove home from a party in Malibu, crashing into a tree and killing himself and his wife instantaneously. Instead of helping her nephews with the loss, goodie-two-shoes Amy hindered them with her incessant nagging, prodding, negativity, and demoralizing comments. How she treated them, I thought, was over the top, even brutal.

However, to this day, Denny says he loves his aunt dearly for taking care of his brother and him. He does agree, though, that she favors Hal. I feel the self-righteous Amy consistently put the screws to my husband. As per Denny, she grated and chastised him regularly, telling him to clean his room, practice his music lessons, always dress or look perfect, or act a certain way.

Not dear Hal. He was her golden boy the minute the court gave her guardianship.

Why couldn't she give them any slack? They no longer had a mom or dad, for goodness' sake.

From the stories I've heard about Amy, I could see why the ol' bat never married—why would anyone fall in love or want to live with her anyway? I know what you're thinking: It's mean of me to believe that, but it shows how much I can't stand the woman. I'm just being honest here. Thanks to modern technology, whether we like it or not, you see my every thought: the good, the bad, and the downright ugly. On the positive side, at least you can't backtrack into my past thoughts, only those in this instant.

Isn't life about having fun, getting what you want, and accomplishing something positive? Do things for you, for your satisfaction, not to please everyone else all the time. Be in control. At least that's my take on life.

Couldn't she stoop low enough to let those boys enjoy something?

I met her for the first time at the restaurant on the golf course on Victory Boulevard, about four months after Denny and I started dating. I never want to step foot in Copperfield's again. Denny had been worried she wouldn't like me. Up to that point, it was as if I had been in one of Denny's shoeboxes, set apart from everyone else in his life, only to open when she wasn't around. No wonder both he and I were tense when I finally met the woman. And get this: Right there, while we're sitting by the window that looks over the eighteenth green, she stops to pray for her food. How embarrassing! Everyone must have been staring at us ... at me. I smiled and looked down; I had no clue what else to do. Next, she was preaching, ranting, and going on about stuff I've never heard of or care about—you should do this, don't do this, you need to do that, blah, blah, blah. *Bunk*, I say. Total *bunk*.

As she continued her proselytizing, I smiled and nodded as I ate my club sandwich with no mayo and a side of fries, knowing that Denny had told me to nod, agree with her, and keep showing my pearly whites. He pegged that one right.

What a way to ruin lunch.

Do you get the picture I'm painting of her? Sound familiar to anyone you know? How did you handle the person? A piece of work, huh?

During the forty minutes that seemed like hours of trying to reboot a complex computer program without instructions, she was on her religious pulpit declaring how poorly the world runs and ranting about evil people who are determined to drag it farther into the ground. If it wasn't about today's warped politicians trying to take over our nation, more countries going to war, the latest health outbreak, another school shooting, a malicious cyber-attack, or how morals are worse than when she was a kid, it was how God is in control of her, her dear Hal, Dennis, her son's new girlfriend (you guessed it, me), and the silly salad she was feebly picking. Everything, good or bad, has a purpose, has a reason. Yep, I've got a minor in psychology, and she was telling me she knows all about how people are, the meaning of life, and—if such exists—the hereafter. I say all religion or afterlife beliefs are a bunch of hocus-pocus nonsense that people lean on as a crutch because they're too insecure and inadequate to believe in themselves.

Sure. Whatever, woman.

You agree with me, don't you? Tell me you don't believe in all that God stuff, especially in today's chaotic world where who knows what will happen around the next corner.

I admit I was angry then, but I also was afraid; she made me nervous and does to this day, four years later. Forever walking on eggshells, I can't please her. I can't win with her. I must put my guard up continually. Do I want to?

Would you?

Should I try to play her games?

Nope, not me. And neither should Denny.

Denny once told me he married me because I was like his mother and aunt. I'm fine being like his mom; apparently, she was thoughtful, loving, and had a sharp mind. But being similar to Amy? Oh, no. Please, no! He's right that we're both independent thinkers and doers, but that's where the similarity stops. I don't want to be opinionated or domineering like her, although she may think I am. Who knows—you may even believe that.

Okay, I'm not perfect, but I'm a good person. I don't intentionally break the law or hate people so much that I want to hunt them down with an AK-47 or strap a bomb to myself and explode in a sports stadium. Yes, I usually get my way because, I admit, I sometimes have to manipulate others to prove a point or accomplish my goal. I always do it for a good reason.

I'm a twenty-eight-year-old, college-educated woman with a master's in journalism working for the *Valley News* in Los Angeles. My success comes from putting years of well-planned knowledge, effort, and sweat into my vocation. I did it myself and am accomplished. I've arrived, and I neither like nor appreciate anyone stepping in my way or on my toes.

You get my type: I know what I'm doing, am confident, learn things only I'm interested in, stay logical no matter what's happening around me, and don't need anyone telling me anything. If I want to learn something, I'll research it myself and not be told what's what. I must have order and consider everything pertinent that's going on around me. Honestly, I must get my way in every situation and circumstance that I can control. I may do things differently than you, but usually, I win. Like it or not, I'm not changing for anyone, anywhere, or anyway, especially for that bat! I'm not like her. And no, I won't change for you, either. Sorry, you heard it from me directly; you'll find that I'm blunt about my opinions.

Using the side of a sharp knife, I carefully chip away at the burnt cheese on the edges of the lasagna pan, determined to let my anger subside toward her and my unobservant husband. How dare he take her side! Especially if I guess what could be happening to me is true. He has no clue, and I want to keep it that way.

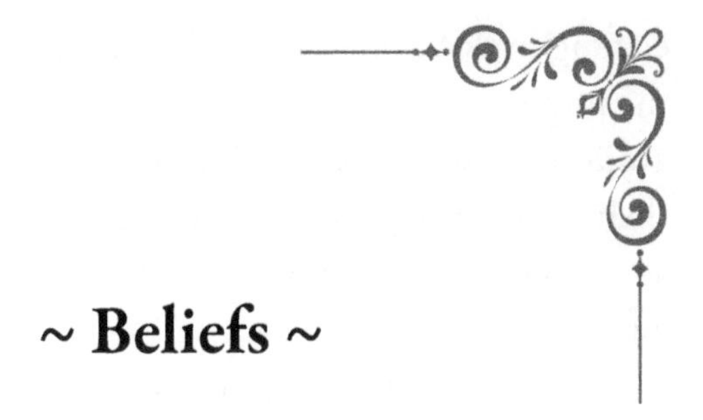

~ Beliefs ~

I let the pan soak in the sink, grab a dish towel to wipe down the kitchen island's countertop, and restack the drink coasters that we used at dinnertime. Returning to the sink and rinsing off a wine glass, I set it upside down on a neatly spread-out hand towel.

After making sure the rest of the kitchen looks worthy of a magazine cover, I turn my attention back to my husband. Where is he? I look around the corner of the great room to the stairs that lead to Denny's office and the bedrooms; I check to see if the door is still closed. As I expected, it is.

Being upset with Amy is not the crux of my problem. It's multifaceted, and here's why: After I'd gotten home from work early and before dinner tonight, Amy stopped by for a few minutes. Only a few minutes, thank goodness. Amazing how fast she can ruin a day.

Because of the current legal changes in our state, she wanted to give Denny a copy of her living will that her lawyer had redrawn due to new restricted laws about passing on property to others and the tax implications. She was barely inside the house before she started sermonizing.

The main thing she emphasized was that I have no morals (which none of us does, so that includes you, too). Before coming to that point, it was all about Heaven, Hell, salvation, the forgiveness of sins—you know, vague topics Denny and I avoid discussing. She said I'm sinful and need to repent, but there was nothing she could do about it; she said something about "love the sinner but hate the sin." Back on her religious gig.

My father hammered into me to always stand up for my beliefs, as they are the most important thing a person has. So, I took his wise advice, telling her flatly to get off her soapbox and stop evangelizing all the time.

Well, that's where the problem started. I told Amy she should bend her pious, stupid rules, and this is who I am, and she had better accept me as is, because I'm not changing for her or her God or anyone. And, for your information, my morals are perfectly fine. I'm a good person overall, as I'm sure you are, too.

My words didn't go over well, as next she turned to my husband and said in a timid tone, "Dennis, you still believe in God, don't you? You know He's alive and in your heart?"

Denny muttered, his eyes taking on that deer-in-the-headlights look, "Yeah, Aunt Amy, and I know He'll never leave me or forsake me."

I will tell you and only you that Denny is such a patsy. He's never said something that blatant before in my presence. "Religion is a private thing" has always been his response, and I've let it go at that. But to say he believes in God and a deity of some kind will always be with him? Excuse me, that's not my Denny. Over the last several days, I've noticed his attitude has changed. His words came out of nowhere. Who did I marry?

Why does his aunt have this grasp on him that he cowers to every time? What's with him? Do you have any idea?

When Amy abruptly left, her last words were that she'd pray for us. Okay, lady, do whatever you want, including praying, but please don't get me personally involved.

Since only I had wine tonight, I carry the now washed and dried glass to the curio cabinet and open the top hutch, being careful not to clink it against my grandmother's antique tea set. I glance up the staircase to the closed door again. No movement, no sounds.

As I said before, I'm as good as the next person; I mess up here and there, but I'm a decent human. It's not like I've broken the Ten Commandments—"thou shalt not kill; thou shalt not steal; thou shalt not commit adultery." I'm a law-abiding citizen.

I'm so tired of it. I'm tired of her interrupting our lives. At this point, for some reason, I'm on the verge of crying, mainly out of frustration and exhaustion, so don't be surprised if I do.

After the disturbing lady left, Denny and I had a fight during dinner. He and I said hurtful words to each other. I won't go into the details, as I don't think it's proper for me to rehash them, especially to you, someone I don't know. I'm confused, hurt, and upset. I don't understand anymore.

My eyes tear up as I try to remain resolute and composed; I twist the hand towel, straighten it out again, and repeat the process before finally returning it to its holder next to the fridge. Of course, I double-check to make sure no wrinkles show on it.

Do you think I overreacted to Amy's self-righteous sermon? Should I go upstairs and apologize to Denny? You may think I should be the first to admit fault, but that's not me. I rarely feel it's necessary to say I'm sorry; I don't do regrets either.

Due to my surprisingly emotional state, I'm probably overworked and exhausted.

What do you think? It'll be all right, won't it? Denny and I will patch things up, right?

Amy praying or not, my marriage will stay intact. Especially now.

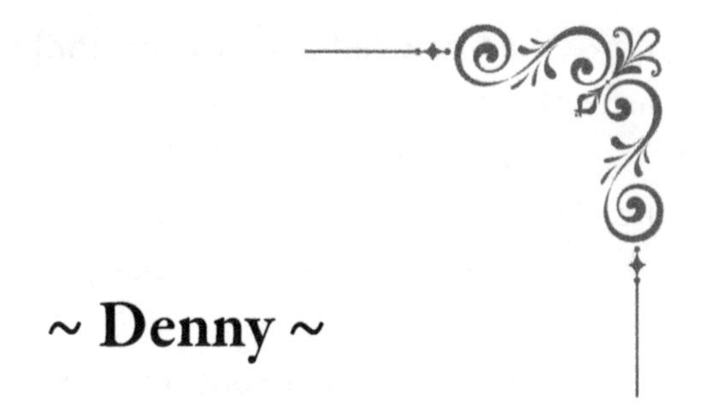

~ Denny ~

Considered to be one who's logical, I rationalize the situation.

Hear me out.

I shouldn't be mad at Amy. It should be Denny.

Opening the dishwasher, I put a serving spoon in its proper slot. I hate when anyone puts plates backward in a machine. Especially if it's my machine. Silverware's another big issue. Point them down in the trays, not up, to get a proper cleaning. You'd stab yourself if you did it the other way. Don't people think?

I rinse out a small dish towel and start wiping down the range for the third time. I'm fanatical about it looking clean, with no caked or baked-on food on the grates. Tell me I have issues with OCD, tell me I'm anal-retentive and need to chill and relax. Remember, this is me—this is how I am. Let me get inside your head and see what's in there. Will I roll my eyes at you like you just did to me?

When I met Denny at UCLA, he was finishing his degree in marketing, and I was a sophomore taking photos for the college paper. Since part of my job was to capture the fun, I naturally saw a lot of him. Of course, I took plenty of shots of him being on intramural basketball and baseball teams. But it took me a year and a particularly thrilling baseball game to maneuver our relationship into a hot, steamy romance.

At first, my friend, Rochelle, did the writing, and I did the picture-taking. Thanks to her falling in love and quitting school, I took over both tasks. But photojournalism remains my first love, my avocation.

Denny isn't stellar at confrontation or debate; I think it's due to living with Aunt Amy during his teen years. As you may have noticed, I'm the competitive and even-keeled one.

During our fight twenty minutes ago, he ticked me off when he said frankly that I'm mean and calculated, especially toward his aunt. Well, that's a snarky comment. What is with him these days? He doesn't debate or confront his aunt, and he keeps his trap shut, yet he confirms Amy's observation that I'm heartless, cruel to others, and a sinner. Excuse me? I correct myself—no, he had added, "All of us, including you, Sarah, are not perfect, and we're born with a sinful nature." He must have borrowed Amy's podium for that remark.

By the end of the argument, at least he admitted he had his faults when I called him on the carpet about his confronting issues.

Okay, I do have problems, I agree. I'm not perfect all the time. Are you? Doubt it. You can admit to me that you mess up from time to time. We both may be good people with minor flaws, and that's a part of life.

Not perfect? Denny kept saying, "inside," "inside our hearts," and "inside our minds." Secrets we keep deep down "inside" us. Bad thoughts, bad ideas, bad schemes.

I've got plenty of secrets inside me, especially at this minute. Don't you? Doesn't everyone? Be honest here. It's just the two of us. You are keeping something hidden, too, I know it. Same with bad ideas: You get upset when the driver in the car behind you flips you off when you cut in front of him, and you have visions of slamming your brakes so you can say to your insurance agent, "Why, he rear-ended me." Or how about pocketing work pens that aren't yours? Bet you do that occasionally, too, thinking you deserve them. Do you fantasize about having sex with someone, even if you're married? Come on, admit it.

You and I are the same. We're not perfect all the time. No one can be; we're human after all. It's normal.

See, if you're honest about it, you'll agree with me.

I look up and stare outside the kitchen window above the sink, pondering this sinful nature I supposedly have. Two little girls are playing in the blissful California evening. The sun is over the San Fernando Valley hills to the west, and the air is breezy and pleasant. The ideal time of day, the perfect time to take a walk. The cute girls are on the playground's swing set, going back and forth like pendulums, giggling away. Maybe they're pretending they can fly as they soar through the air.

A flicker of sadness overwhelms me.

Something's wrong.

Something's not right.

Something needs to be resolved.

Time to face the music, girl.

Oh, please help me get through what I'm about to do next. Please, I need your help.

~ Secret ~

I've put it off as long as I must. It's inevitable. Time to prove what I know.

You're here, so come with me. I prefer not to share my upcoming discovery with you, but it looks like we have no other choice.

Going over to my oversized camera bag on the floor by the half-moon mahogany table near our front door, I pass by the stairs and look upward. Is Denny still mad at me or is he merely concentrating on sales-commission spreadsheets?

Pulling my bag open, I quietly retrieve the small oblong box, palm it in my hand, and head to our downstairs half-bath tucked next to the staircase. Slipping inside the room, all-white except for the same dark wood flooring that's everywhere but the two upstairs bathrooms, I turn on the fan and light switches, knowing the fan's sound produces a relentless, high-pitched, metal-on-metal screech. We need to get it fixed; it drives everyone who uses that bathroom crazy. But for the moment, the loud clanging will mask any possibility of Denny knowing what I'm doing.

Behind me, I lock the door, a rarity in my routine. After lifting my shirt, unbuttoning my jeans, and pulling down my underwear, I sit down on the opened toilet seat, trying not to notice a chip in the dark purple nail polish on my big toe. Reading the step-by-step instructions on the box, I ignore the words mentioning the test works best in the morning. I zero in on the little pee-stained white plastic stick and check the second hand of my Seiko watch. It keeps ticking and ticking. The time takes forever.

I wonder, but I know the truth. I feel it inside me. As the little straight line slowly merges into a plus sign, I learn my fate.

I'm pregnant.

Sure, you're thinking the marker's reading it wrong since it's evening, not morning. It must be a mistake. Please, just this once.

Barely nodding my head back and forth, I let out a quiet, hopeless sigh followed by a whispered cuss word that seems more pronounced than the clattering fan above my head.

Life's never perfect. Life's never planned. Things happen. There are consequences. As Denny says, "Everything has a reason." Sure.

After I put the used stick and instructions back in the box, I rest it on the counter, clean up, and re-dress. I look at myself in the mirror as I wash my hands with decorative soap in the shape of a sea urchin, and rinse and dry them on the nearby hand towel. My unemotional posture forces my determined movements to be automatic.

I muse. You know, I've heard the television commercials saying one out of four women read that silly stick wrong. Maybe I'm one of them. Would you be able to read it correctly?

Tomorrow I'll get another box and test again, but this time I'll do it the second I get out of bed, making some lame excuse so Denny doesn't question why I'm spending more time than usual in the bathroom. Maybe I didn't do it correctly or wait for the right amount of time to pass. Think so?

No, I know I'm pregnant.

Picking up the used product, I crunch it tightly in my hand, wanting to squeeze away the plus and turn it into a negative. I close my eyes in frustration and rest my back against the wall that's opposite the sink, allowing my bare feet to slide onto the plush rug so my body drifts down to the floor.

I'm pregnant.

Do I want to be?

What do you think? Have you been pregnant? What was it like? What should I expect?

What have I done?

It's my stupid fault for forgetting to use contraception when we took that weekend trip to Santa Barbara three weeks ago. It was an early celebration of our second wedding anniversary; I thought it wouldn't be a problem.

What do you think I should do?

I bet you're jumping to the first conclusion that pops into your head. Stop that train of thought right now, this second!

Yes, of course, it's Denny's child. What kind of person do you think I am? I'm loyal and in love with Denny. And I'm not promiscuous—never expect to be, either, unless my husband does something pathetic, like falls for Brittany, the overly solicitous, flirty, and flighty receptionist at my office who practically drools whenever he happens to stop by the office. Or unless we grow too far apart somehow. Or maybe, I snort, unless I find someone better than him. Zoey, my dear friend, calls finding a replacement "upgrading." You get rid of the clunker car and upgrade to the luxury one as time passes.

Jeremy, a guy at work, comes to mind. He and I clicked right away; we've become good friends because we spend a lot of time together. But I think he wants more than I do. I can't see a physical relationship, only an emotionally growing one.

I guess what I'm saying is Denny's my man, and I hope it stays that way. Do you believe me now?

Having missed my last period, I've been avoiding taking the telling leap to verify or accept the reality.

I don't want Denny to know about the baby.

Denny probably won't know.

And you're not to tell him, either. Keep it to yourself, please.

After getting up off the floor and straightening the rug, I glance at myself in the mirror one last time. My eyes are glistening as a single tear sneaks out, running slowly down my face. I can't tell you why I'm crying, only that I am. It's uncharacteristic of me. I'm feeling an inherent sadness that's unexplainable. I don't want you to see me like this, but there are no words to describe my current emotions.

Wiping the tear away with the back of my hand, I exit the bathroom, tightly clenching the all-telling box and gently holding my stomach.

I wonder if Denny has noticed anything different in me. Has my attitude changed? Did I give anything away at dinner during our argument? Do you think he senses it, too? Do you think I'm acting weird?

Everything's happening too fast.

I didn't expect this and didn't want this.

Am I overwhelmed with female hormones and feelings? Is my body changing, and that's why I'm frustrated, stressed out, and on the hate-Aunt-Amy bandwagon? Ugh.

I reenter the kitchen, open the trash compactor drawer next to the dishwasher, and put all contents of my findings inside. To further hide the evidence, I dig deeper into the bin, lift the mozzarella cheese package that has egg goo smeared on it, and cover the dreaded box. Wishing to forget the truth, I shut the compactor drawer quickly and turn on its compression button, hoping I could change the outcome.

Wishing for other things.

The result's positive.

I don't want this baby.

But Denny does.

Denny has always wanted a baby. He wants several. I want none.

"The fruit of the womb," he jests.

As my mind starts spinning, I open the dishwasher and put in a plastic spatula, then move two plates to the back of the lower rack.

You're here; I need your advice. Is there a way you can tell me what you're thinking? Can you give me any suggestions on what to do next?

There's no reply, which makes me produce an audible sigh.

Okay, let's think this through objectively. My career is launching; I'm getting noticed for my writing and photography. We're doing well financially, but we have the townhouse mortgage, two car payments, credit card debt, and student loans. Now is not the right time. In five or ten years, maybe, but not now. The timing is off. Twenty-eight years old is too young to be a mother.

Denny keeps saying anytime is a good time. Remember, "It happens, and there's a reason." He's convinced that he alone can manage the bills and I don't need to work with his adequate income if we cut back and watch expenses, but in today's volatile economy, I'm skeptical about whether we would make ends meet. He's a commission-based sales representative for audio, video, and computer equipment, so, before COVID, he was on the road often. Now that the virus is manageable and the industry is making a comeback, he's going back to driving around Southern California more often. He'll be spending nights here and there, attending national conventions throughout the year, and sometimes being gone a week at a time. I'll be raising the kid most of the time; I don't want to do it by myself. No thank you. I don't want a child—especially in today's world! I have plenty of time for that later in life when things get more normal. Granted, we're accustomed to the constant barrage of COVID variants, but what about new strains or diseases? How will they affect children?

Amy would want us to have a baby; that's for sure. Dozens of them, so she can implement her cult beliefs and nuances from day one. She can "raise 'em right" in her mind. She'd be over constantly, telling me how to diaper and burp, how to discipline and correct—and how to pray. No thanks.

My parents wouldn't mind more grandkids to coo and cuddle, although they live a state away in Oregon. I don't see them enough, but I think Daddy wouldn't mind having another grandchild.

My sister and her husband, Tom, went through so much red tape to adopt two adorable Korean kids. Silvia would be on my case about my weight and eating and sleeping patterns. In some ways, my only sibling who's older than I am is more protective than Daddy, Mom, Denny, or Amy.

And Mom may be on my side, saying my desires should be put first at this stage in my life. She'd understand I'm young, have years before the maternal clock stops, and could select the child's sex, specific traits, and characteristics. I should wait a few more years until the advanced technology is refined.

But I can't tell my parents right now. They wouldn't understand. Plus, they're coming to visit next week. Maybe I'll tell them then.

What about me? What about my career? Don't I get to make money, even more money than my husband? I'm competitive in everything, especially when it comes to my job.

I don't want to stay at home. I want to be out in society, among my peers. I want to be noticed, particularly at the *Valley News.*

Ever since my photo-and-article report on the governor's son getting killed during a convenience-store robbery, I've been getting accolades at work. Can I be the one who gets to be out and about instead of being stuck at home changing diapers and having barf on my nice clothes? I'm not Silvia and don't want to be. I am Sarah Colton. Women these days can and do demand well-paying, prestigious jobs before and while having children; we're strong enough to decide what we want for ourselves. Mom would agree with me. Do you, too?

Call me the alpha woman and all that women's lib stuff, but don't I get a say in this?

I put both hands on my hips, resolute in my thinking.

I don't want to tell Denny yet. Why should I? He doesn't have to know. Not yet, not this minute. I'm only a few weeks along.

Funny, you're the first to know, yet I don't know your name, age, sex, favorite color, or preferred food. But maybe, somehow, you can help me think through this mess. Can you give me some guidance?

Even so, at this stage, it's barely alive. It doesn't have a name. It's a nobody. I doubt it feels pain, sadness, anxiety, joy, or happiness.

I could get rid of it now and deal with the consequences later, if there are any.

It'll be my little secret. My evil, sinful secret.

I shut the dishwasher door with additional firmness.

Keep it to myself for now. Don't tell anyone—it's our secret. No one else needs to know.

And please don't question me right now.

Why? Because I say so ... I'm sensible. I'm in control of my body. Tomorrow I'll go back to work, and I'll give it a day or two before I tell Denny or do anything rash. Everything will be fine; you'll see.

Everything will go back to normal in a week or two.

Everything.

~ Hal ~

I must get out of this funk. Too much to deal with in my head, especially since you're in there as well. Too many things to think about every minute of the day. I'm caught up in a whirlwind of emotions—of frustrations with too many people, including my husband. Maybe myself, too.

Do you feel that way sometimes? Like you can't get a grasp on everything going around you? Do you think life is careening by, and you can't stop the Ferris wheel for a few seconds to pause and do absolutely nothing? To simply shut down?

"Denny?" I call up to the second floor of the townhouse. I should break the non-communication first, but why bother? He won't answer; he's probably still mad at me. He stormed off after our spat without helping me clean up the dinner dishes and went upstairs to his hallowed office, slamming the door for emphasis.

He loves to spend hours there, working on sales reports, purchase orders, commission statements, texts, and emails and connecting with all his company and social networks online. He'll put on his high-end headphones and crank up his state-of-the-art, high-definition stereo system complete with the latest ultra-modern audio gadgets and wireless cable connections. Using his father's reconditioned turntable with ancient LP record albums, he escapes to the musical world of 1960s and 1970s classic rock. Go figure that he'd go back to that era and the same music his father appreciated, especially the Beatles, Cream, and Iron Butterfly—not like the supposed garbage I ask Alexa to play throughout our house or listen to on my Bluetooth in my car.

When we were stuck at home during the COVID shutdown, we painted the walls dusty green and added a dark cherry wood desk and matching cabinets with an oatmeal-colored shaggy rug and brown leather executive chair. It's his room, not mine. English golf clubs, including an old niblick, mashey, and antique putter, hang on the wall beside the framed photos of Denny's trip to Pebble Beach years ago with John, his golfing buddy who's a police officer. Golf balls with handwritten accomplishments line up neatly in a hanging rack with matching dark green chairs on each side. It's his haven. He loves the comfort the four walls give him, as it's where he spends most of his time when he's not on the road working, which he has gotten used to since sales and service had to be done via video conferencing during the pandemic.

The office has a jack-and-jill bathroom connected to the second bedroom farther down the hall; a mini darkroom is set up in its walk-in closet where I also keep my photography equipment and coin collections. The bedroom is not fancy like the office; it's done in tans and whites similar to the kitchen and great room. A large blown-up photograph I took of a silhouetted lifeguard station at sunset at the Santa Monica Pier is above the bed with a dozen of my black-and-white pictures identically sized and framed flanking another wall. Simple room, nothing spectacular, only functional. Like me.

I don't dare go up the stairs and check on him. What if he found out about my condition? I don't want to start another argument.

The door remains shut as always when he's in there.

As I mentioned, he's been acting peculiarly the past few days. I don't want to ask him what has set him off; I have no interest right now in dealing with more drama.

Noticing my smartphone ding, I wipe my hands on another towel, swing my leg around to sit on the island's barstool, and tap the start-up button to view what's new.

Ah, the all-present world of electronic connections comes to life. Ever since Meta launched its AI Research SuperCluster supercomputer, going online to search for anything is faster and easier than it was mere months ago. State your name aloud on your phone and let it start searching; you'll find there're only a few things it doesn't know about you. So much for privacy. At least only you can read my mind right now, not a computer. Yet.

Checking my emails, I run through the recent additions. Let's see ... three from my boss; another from Lily, a gal at work who tries hard to be kind to me; one that looks like a joke from Daddy that will be deleted; and one notification of a post on my Facebook account.

I've never been a fan of Facebook, Snapchat, Instagram, Twitter, TikTok, or any other kind of social media, and I'm less likely to be than ever since Silvia is on a quest to post every stage of her children's lives. Denny has embraced social networking with vigor. He's into staying connected with his pals from college as well as from his private high school. To think how thrilled he was when friends from his Boy Scout days contacted him—come on, we're talking friends when he was eight years old? Like I care what those people from back then do now? How do they relate to me? Honestly, I burned enough bridges in high school not to merit any friends. They and high school mean zilch to me now.

Do you have a social media account? If so, how many friends are on it? I ask sarcastically, like it decides how socially acceptable you are. Or should I ask you to friend me? No, sorry. No interest there.

Denny has over a thousand connected friends on Facebook, eight hundred on Twitter, and two hundred on LinkedIn. My Facebook account has fewer than twenty, including Denny, his brother, Silvia, Tom, and some of Mom's distant relatives. I must have over five hundred on LinkedIn, as it's more of a professional site for job-seeking. In case anything happens to me at the *Valley News,* I keep my online resume up to date. Denny teases me, saying that because he has more connections, he's more popular than I am. Fine, another point for Denny-boy. Big deal. I say it's a waste of time, telling people what you're doing every thirty seconds. Get real, fake friends. I prefer to spend my time in better ways.

However, I have found interesting things on these types of sites when I browse through Denny's friends, like his old girlfriends, teachers, and coworkers he hangs out with occasionally.

Do you search the Web for old friends and flames of yours or your loved ones? Tell me; I certainly will not and cannot spill the beans. Is stalking one of the secrets that obsess you?

However, one can learn a lot about a person online.

Take Hal. Denny's brother loves social media; he's the one to blame for Denny getting involved in it.

Hal says it's the best way to connect with multiple people at one time without having to do a ton of work. Having more than four thousand connections, he keeps in touch—yeah, that's a fact. One comment on his page and everyone knows where he is and what he's doing.

I click on Facebook and go to my main page: There are three new photos of Silvia and Tom's Jack and Jasmine and one from Hal.

The younger bro is weird but nice, with the flare of a vagabond. You never know what to expect from him, in a good way. He says he's a wanderer, but I'd call him a gypsy. As I mentioned, he's two years younger than Denny, so he's my age but single. He hasn't settled down; he's been gallivanting around the world, enjoying life to the fullest. Currently, he's somewhere in Israel working at a language school, teaching Hebrew students how to read, write, and speak English. Good, solid, help-society guy and job. Of course, Amy calls him her "old-fashioned missionary."

And yes—you guessed it—he has the same religious fervor his aunt has.

Take that knowledge with a grain of salt.

I must hand it to him; he doesn't preach at you like the one and only Ms. Colton. He acts, not talks. He's more subtle and not obnoxious, the type who stays out of your hair and life but is firm in his beliefs. Don't you respect people like that, who are faithful to their beliefs but not pushing them onto others?

Look at this photo of Israel's Western Wall and Hal's post:

In Jerusalem. Very cool experience today! With the recent call for a bona fide peace treaty that may have some traction this time, Michael and I had the opportunity to go with an Islamic mullah into the underground tunnels under the Temple Mount, which was quite interesting. We were shown recently made replicas of the Old Testament vessels, pottery, dishes, and musical instruments to be used in the rebuilt Temple. Yes, for when the sacrifices are re-established! Unbelievable. All in gold, silver, and brass, beautifully designed. Sorry, we're not allowed to take pictures inside. I will post more later. Also, I'm having a wonderful time teaching. God is good. Love and miss you!

Now that is interesting. It's history; I love history. To think that the Jews and Arabs may have real peace soon is a wonderful prospect. Plus, they're remaking articles to use when the Jewish tabernacle is rebuilt. Cool. No temple yet, and I don't know how or when it'll be rebuilt in that part of the world, but it seems the forever hatred of the Jews and the endless attempt at a peace treaty between Israel and other nations may finally be resolved.

I'll believe the parts of the Bible that archeologists can verify, mostly Old Testament information like cities, artifacts, and historical events, but not much else. Some of those stories have to be allegorical or make-believe. Prove to me there was a flood, the parting of a sea, or the resurrection of Jesus, a mere prophet during His day. Go on, let's debate, and you prove it to me. Try me.

I accidentally click on one of Hal's friend's responses to his post.

Up comes: *For the wages of sin is death; but the gift of God is eternal life through Jesus Christ our Lord.* Romans 6:23.

Oops.

Didn't mean to click on a Bible verse.

Wait. Let me think this through. I'm analytical enough to read this without getting all worked up, like Amy's fire-and-brimstone attitude. Ah, a challenge. Or should I say a pregnant lady who's in control of her hormones? That's how I should start approaching issues. Pregnant and emotionally charged. Are you ready?

Here goes: "The wages of sin is death"—so it's saying that I must pay because I sin? And then there's this gift from God that gives eternal life. Okay, what does that mean? Denny said all have sinned, that even I sin. Okay, got that far, and have admitted I'm not perfect. Neither is Denny. Neither is Amy. Neither are you. Don't understand the "wages" issue. If I work, I get paid. If I sin, the payment I get is my death? Payment for my sin is that I die?

Well, everyone dies, right? There's no afterlife. Why would I die because I sin?

But God offers a gift that's supposedly eternal life. A gift is free, with no strings attached, meaning I don't do anything for it. Although I'm dead from this sin stuff, there's life. An eternal life, although I'm dead. Unclear, confusing verse. Looks like Bible jargon to me unless I was in seminary and studied it.

To be honest, I've never seriously thought about Heaven versus Hell. I don't believe in either one. When you die, you die. There may be a Superior Being who created it all at one point, and we evolved, but I'd have to say I'm stuck somewhere between atheism and agnosticism.

Do you think that way? Or are you a Jesus person? Well, as my dad would say, "To each his own."

Life here on earth is a one-time-through buffet; you pick and choose what you want, what you need, and what makes you happy. Metaphorically, take the salad, the prime rib, some au gratin, or mac and cheese, fill up on some desserts—then you die. That's it; no going back for seconds. You're the one in control of your life, not someone else, some so-called Superior Being. And no Hell. Who and why would there be a God who creates a Hell? He isn't an all-loving God if He made an eternal pit of fire for bad people.

The devil, demons, Hitler—bad, bad people, but not ordinary people. Not someone like me. Or maybe you. We're good people.

I believe God, if He exists, would never make a Hell, especially for eternity. The concept of Heaven may be a little more conceivable or ideological, but Hell seems too harsh. Trust me, I'm not horrible enough to deserve such a place. I doubt that you are, either.

I'm unsure whether there's a God. Maybe Someone or Something had to create the massive universe—but a God to whom people are to bow to regularly? A God we pray to for redemption or so that we're not sick or poor or whatever meets our next need or fancy? Makes no sense to me. Thus it can't be true.

Then there's this new-age spiritualism my sister believes in. You know, the teaching Oprah Winfrey touted years ago that God is everywhere in the universe and within us. From what

I understand, it's based on Taoism and Hinduism; the main point is since God is everywhere and in everything, we can aspire to become a god within ourselves. With many flocking to the occult with its cosmic energy, chakras, and crystals, I'd rather believe in her thinking than Amy's unrealistic, hard-core beliefs. If I work at it, I can become a god, and so can you. I'd consider that belief system. It's all about me, an individual, like it should be.

Well, religion or no religion, I'm in control here and now, and that's all that matters.

The little girls are still swinging back and forth outside the window. They look like sisters.

Thinking about sisters, mine is strong-willed, independent, and knows what she wants. Silvia is only eighteen months older than I am, but she often acts like she's my mother. Once when we were young and eating at the dinner table, she flatly refused to eat peas. Daddy ran after her with a spoon full of them, spilling them all over the place. Banished from the table, she spent time in her room for the night. The next time we had peas, she snuck them in her napkin and jammed them under the table's corner, only to have Daddy retrieve them later. He grounded her for a week without the Internet.

Silvia got her degree in art but never used it professionally. After she married Tom, they moved to Florida, where she works for an independent insurance agency that specializes in homeowner, automobile, and healthcare policies. Tom has worked for his father's construction business near Orlando since he was a teen, and he now owns it, so he keeps quite busy.

When Silvia and Tom found out they couldn't get pregnant (he had some hereditary issues with strange medical names I won't attempt to look up or pronounce for you), she researched every possible option, and it took two years to find those two precious, parentless siblings. Somehow amid COVID, Silvia and Tom caught a red-eye flight to Korea to get the babies and have enjoyed every second since they took them into their arms. Silvia would do anything in the world for them, and so would Tom. My sister is one hopeful person—even more so with her newfound beliefs. But I'm not like her; having a baby would make me miserable.

Do you have siblings? I've told you about Denny's and mine. Are yours younger or older? Have a good relationship with them? How I wish you could respond to me. It would connect us instead of being one-sided.

Letting out a sigh, I question why I'm the only one here using my brain but not getting anywhere.

What's wrong with me? Should I be thinking about this thing, this child, inside me, instead of spiritual, philosophical, or relative-related mumbo jumbo?

As my mind jumps from topic to topic randomly, I wonder what I've gotten myself into this time.

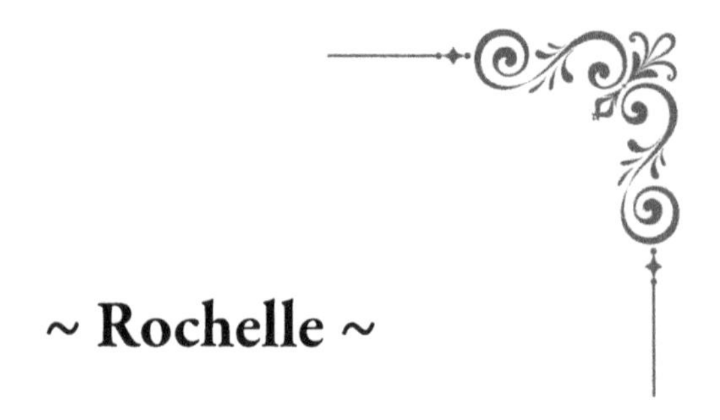

~ Rochelle ~

Realizing once again there's nothing earth-shattering on the Internet, I close my phone's server, slip off the bar stool, and enter the great room where we have a matching cream-colored couch and loveseat surrounded by glass tables and situated on a rug with brown and sage-green designs. The wide wood shelf in our bay window houses seven prized orchids that I've collected and babied for years. You watch me aimlessly check each plant, removing any dead leaves and sticking my finger in the pots to evaluate the moisture. Two of the plants are huge and in bloom with pure-white flowers; they're currently looking healthy and gorgeous. Do you like them, too, or are you the type who doesn't want to deal with the upkeep of indoor plants?

And, if you are curious, yes, I am still ignoring my husband. He deserves my inattention. This is how we play our marital volley when we disagree—we avoid each other at all costs until we cool down.

I retreat to the kitchen again, passing the double-sided fireplace wall separating the great room from our dining area. I pull out a water pitcher from a bottom cupboard and rest it in the sink opposite the side with the soaking lasagna pan. As the container fills with water, I notice the girls are still on the swings, going back and forth, back and forth, not a care in the world. At least they no longer have to wear face masks outside or at school. It's been cathartic for everyone since the CDC eased the mask-wearing mandate.

How I wish I were like these cute girls; I'm jealous of their innocence, ignorance, and lightheartedness. Wouldn't it be wonderful to be a kid again?

When the pitcher is full, I head back to the bay window, carefully pouring water on my treasured plants, making sure no moisture gets on the Alexa unit or security camera that faces outward to our front door entry walkway and semi-enclosed patio. The patio is enclosed by a low-profile privacy fence with a matching gate that is usually kept open. The area is furnished with a wrought-iron table and two matching chairs where Denny and I often have coffee at on weekends.

As I explained earlier, Rochelle was on the journalism team with me at UCLA where all our articles were submitted online. We roomed together one semester, but it was sometimes trying on our relationship to be in each other's face day and night, especially on top of the many venues we covered on campus. We tended to stay up most nights discussing each day's ins and outs that didn't matter. Talk about lack of sleep, rooming with Rochelle was detrimental to our well-being. We had a special friendship back then.

Rochelle started dating Dave during the middle of our first year, and the relationship quickly escalated. She was obsessed and so in love with him that she practically stopped going to class. He wasn't in journalism but was a pre-med major who was a neat freak (it was obvious that Rochelle and I were not, but, trust me, I've gotten better after being married to Denny).

Dave, a few years older and no doubt wiser, swept Rochelle off her feet, making her crave the whole happily-ever-after concept, complete with a house with a white picket fence and a cute calico cat perched in the window. I used to tease her by saying she'd be chained to being barefoot and pregnant, washing dishes and clothes all day long with her hair up in those huge, old-fashioned curlers. She'd banter that she truly, beyond any doubt, wanted her life in that perfect, rosy way. That's the American way of the 1960s, our parents' Baby-Boomer era. That's true contentment, or so she thought.

Um, no thank you, I say. The idea sounds ultra-dated these days. Would you want to go back and live in that time?

Then came the day Rochelle found out she was pregnant.

Boy, that changed everything.

Dave left her, giving the excuse that he had to fly back East because his grandmother had Alzheimer's and needed him. So, he was out of the picture. Out of her fantasy-filled life.

Rochelle dropped out of the campus newsgroup, giving me the entire intramural sports section to handle.

Rochelle dropped out of school.

Rochelle dropped out of life.

Reality hit her like a concrete boulder.

She had the baby. Joshua David Good. Used her last name, not Dave's.

She tried to move on, grow up, and adjust.

Although we met a couple of times after the baby was born, we don't keep in contact now; all of that changed her too much. She's not even one of my social media friends. No clue how to contact her.

Have you experienced a fallen-apart friendship, too? There's nothing you can do about it, no way of returning to how it once was. I miss her and our fun times. To this day, the loss makes me sad.

Rochelle's bundle of joy wasn't the key to the demise of our relationship; religion was. She was, by genealogy, a Jew, but never promoted it; it had never been an issue between us. She was more apologetic than practicing when it came to her beliefs. It was as though she had curly black hair and I had straight blonde, no big deal between us.

I think when Dave realized she was Jewish, he couldn't handle it since he had come from a strictly Catholic background, so he broke up with her. Never know, maybe his family pressured him to dump her. That's my bet. As far as I knew, after the break-up, Rochelle never talked about Dave, never asked him for support, and never considered him again. I'm not sure if he knows she gave birth to a son; that would be wrong on so many levels.

All because of religious beliefs? Anyone should be able to be married to someone of a different race or religion—what does "all men are created equal" mean? It worked for Denny and me; he was raised Baptist via Amy's insistence, and I had no religious upbringing except to believe in myself. That's a form of religion, don't you think? We're happily married; we have no major problems.

After her baby was born, Rochelle became a Messianic Jew and started pushing her religion on me as Amy does. I don't need any salvation or help in my life. I can do it alone. Rochelle's newfound Christianity may have helped in her time of need, but I don't need any help.

Yet.

I know down inside and do admit that I'm like anyone else. Right now, I don't want help. What I need is affirmation; I need approval.

Will you be one to give it to me, or are you the judgmental type?

Would you change your mind about me if I decide to terminate the baby?

Back to self-absorption—which I'm sure you're tired of, but this is my way of processing problems. This is how my brain functions, although yours may be wired differently. I work the angles until there's nothing left to consider. Leave if you want—you don't have to be here; for all I know, you can leave me and get inside someone else's head if you want. Maybe that one will be more interesting.

Having the baby won't work out the way I want my life to go. It would make a mess of things. I'm not qualified to take care of a newborn and don't want to be a parent right now. I need to know I'm making the right decision for me—not for Denny, you, or anyone else but me. I need approval and assurance. I need to be sure of what I'm doing.

Sure?

No, not really. I'm unsure about the path I'll take. Isn't everyone? We think we will like a job or a person we marry, but we're unsure initially whether we made the right selection. When we make a crucial decision, do we have "buyer's remorse" afterward, wondering if it's truly the right path to take? Isn't that what divorce is, finding out later that you made the wrong choice of a spouse?

What did Rochelle get by making her decision? She could have gotten rid of the baby and kept Dave. I don't know. She chose to keep her baby; she had choices and made that specific one. She's a single parent raising a son and is no longer able to finish her education as she tries to figure out where she'll get the next box of diapers. Sad. I could never raise a child under those circumstances. I must have confidence and purpose.

As I finish watering the last orchid, I consider my options as I play emotional ping-pong in my head.

I should drop it, forget about it, but I can't; it nudges my mind in ways I've never considered. I know you want me to move on, but I can't. This is me, the real me, and how I think inside. I can't stop myself from considering the outcome of my choices.

Am I feeling guilty?

Is that what this is?

Am I feeling sorry for something I may do? Am I feeling shame or remorse?

I don't know; I don't know what I feel.

Empty.

Lost.

Alone.

I have Denny. I have someone who loves me, right?

He'd never understand what I'm feeling. Not now.

Tell me I still have Denny, despite our fight.

~ Mark ~

You must think I'm obsessive-compulsive, and you may be right. But I've got one more section of the puzzle to add.

I head back into the kitchen, dumping the residual water in the sink. I dry off the pitcher with a hand towel and put it back in its place. Next, I press the "Order" button on the fridge and verbally request the Alexa unit to add a bottle of shiraz, the wine I opened earlier, to our shopping list.

Speaking of electronics, we have too many of them. Because of Denny's job, he insists we have and use the latest inventions available. Not only are Wi-Fi-enabled listening devices in all rooms except the bathrooms, but also there are smart televisions, smart cellphones, smart kitchen appliances, smart beds, smart watches, smart vehicles, and smart security cameras in our possession, plus—if you can believe it—smart audio sunglasses and smart clothing. Say the word, and these things come to life and obey our every command and demand. Yes, we're well-connected to the Internet to make our lives easier and more organized. Sometimes it's overwhelming, as I constantly must ask my husband how to do things with them.

Denny loves trying them out and playing with their features—says they're great innovations that keep getting better as he walks around with earbuds all day long, speaking to his clients allegedly they're in front of him. He's the reason you are in my head right now; when his company was approached by a start-up looking for test subjects for their new mind-reading AI program, he convinced me to participate in it, and I agreed, mainly because the company pays you to do it. Surely, there is no harm to me in you being here, right?

And get this: Last week, the newly released multiverse hologram system arrived, so Mark, another salesperson at Denny's company, and he have been tinkering with it. It's so real, it's bizarre. When I first saw it in action, I thought Mark had flown into town and was upstairs in the office, chatting away about the last Consumer Electronics Show in Las Vegas. I rarely enter Denny's office—his chamber, his asylum—as if it's holy ground. When I tapped on the door and entered the room, I had to do a double take, because it looked like Mark was sitting in one of the wingback chairs. Then the two of them duped me by having Mark reach out to hug me. Scared me to death when I grabbed nothing but air and realized he wasn't there in person. Creepy real. Have you seen or used a visual holoporter yet?

Back to the topic, let me tell you about Mark.

Nice guy but has issues like all of us. I only mention him because he went through quite an ordeal.

You see me open the nearby junk drawer that holds everything from batteries and phone chargers to rubber bands, small used votive candles, and rolled paper holders for coins. The drawer is an issue between my husband and me. He wants it cleaned out and most of its contents dumped in the trash; unfortunately, I continue to add odds and ends to it.

Mindlessly I sort through it, hoping to discard a couple of useless items.

Here's Mark's story: He's several years older than Denny and has been working with the company for over eight years. He covers the Arizona and Nevada territory while Denny covers Southern California. Mark and Denny get along fine since they're not competing for the same clients or commissions. Often the company has contests and quotas, forcing the two to be competitive for bonuses and rewards, but there's nothing wrong with that in the corporate sales world. Denny enjoys it when Mark comes to town for meetings. The two have a good, solid friendship.

Mark and his wife, Melissa, live in Tucson, Arizona. Guess they've been together for at least ten years. Like us, they moved in together before they got married, trying to get used to being able to put up with each other. Good, moral people. Amy would interject that we're big-time sinners, fornicators who ignored the marriage bed, but who let her be the judge? These days, everyone—straight or gay or whatever—shacks up before a major commitment like marriage, and some never marry. No big deal, it's the way it works nowadays. Trial run, so you don't divorce later.

Years ago, Melissa got pregnant—this was before they had tied the knot. So, Mark decided it was the right thing to do to propose to her at the Rose Bowl football game in Pasadena. Yes, the one with a zillion people in attendance. This was before COVID hit, and the stadium was packed to the max. And, if that isn't the most unromantic thing ever, they got married during the Masters golf tournament the same year. I know, not romantic, but if you knew Mark, sports and romance are the highlights of his life. I'm surprised he didn't arrange to be married at Augusta National, right in the "Amen Corner" on the golf course. They married during the tournament, not at it, and, of course, not during Sunday's final eighteen holes. Who said golf isn't a silly sport?

Everyone thought everything was going great with Melissa's pregnancy, except when she went to the doctor at the beginning of her second trimester and found out the baby would have Down's syndrome. No history on either side; it appeared out of nowhere.

Mark was devastated. He wanted Melissa to abort the fetus due to its imperfections, but she refused. He told us he couldn't deal with a child who may have multiple disabilities; he wasn't cut out for it and wouldn't know how to raise him or her, let alone pay for the medical expenses.

Although I never pegged her as being religious, Melissa kept saying God had her get pregnant, so He would help them with this, no matter how many defects the child had. She stayed strong while Mark crumbled with the expectancy of the newborn. Melissa won.

Matilda, or "Matty" as they called her, was born with disabilities due to abnormal chromosomes, a severe case, complete with small, odd-shaped ears, wide-set eyes, and an undeveloped heart. One could easily tell, by looking at the newborn, that there was something wrong. From the second she was born, the neonatal ward was Matty's home.

Mark and Melissa stayed beside her incubator every minute, exhausted, as they prayed, begged, cried, and wished for a miracle.

The poor child died six days after she was born ... never to grow up, go to school, marry, or have children.

I know, I'm cheery here, telling you all this. Sorry for the downer.

Maybe it was best for both Mark and Melissa, but to this day, I don't understand it. How could God make parents go through such anguish? That is if there is a God.

And what if that happens to me?

Would I abort the baby if I found out it has the wrong number of chromosomes? Or would I keep it, taking care of it day and night as it suffered—as I would suffer? It would alter the many plans I have for my life. What if it's defective due to all the COVID vaccinations Denny and I have had? I've been reading nightmare stories recently about what many medicines could now be doing to our bodies.

So, I worry. What about this inside me? Is it healthy? Are there any problems with it that I should know about?

Can you help me stop worrying about everything that's going on?

My fingers find a metal bottle opener in the junk drawer, so I move it to the drawer near the oven range that holds our wine and beer paraphernalia. Next, I locate an elastic hair band; you notice me pulling wayward strands of hair out of my face, securing them in a ponytail with the band. Much better.

I continue my train of thought.

After the draining funeral with the tiny casket and lots of pink roses, life went on with Mark and Melissa, and they still have no children.

In talking to her from time to time, Melissa rarely mentions Matty, God, or the thought of getting pregnant again. For months, she stayed consistent, impassive, and had a "forge-forward" attitude and appearance.

Mark didn't. He drank, and a lot. According to Melissa, one time she found him sitting in the dark in their master bedroom closet, balled up in the corner among his shoe collection, crying. Then he drank some more. We're not talking about a casual glass of wine here and there, but hard drinks and pot. Addiction took over. For over two years, Mark was not there, not happy, and not functioning. Dennis and I noticed his dark moods, anger issues, and permanent puffy circles under his red, glassy eyes. When Melissa found a bottle of Jack Daniels hidden in the back of their master bathroom toilet tank, she confronted him and gave him an ultimatum: alcohol or her.

Because he loved her so much, including when he was in his stupor, he went to AA meetings and some other class and did a complete one-eighty. He stopped drinking, ceased being in his blue mood, and suddenly snapped out of it. Just like that! The fastest withdrawal program I've ever seen.

A whole new guy.

This abrupt change happened two months ago. When I saw Mark last month on a Zoom call, he looked and acted entirely different. It seemed that a new person had entered the body we knew as Mark. He told Denny when they were evaluating that hologram program on Tuesday how happy he was now that he and Melissa had found what they had been looking for all this time. He invited Denny to an online seminar coming up next week that has in-person classes here in the Valley, and Denny promised he would either watch it or go to one. For Denny to promise anything to anybody (unless of course, it's Aunt Amy or, sometimes, me) took me by surprise. It must have impressed my husband to see such a sudden, for-the-better change in Mark.

In the drawer I'm digging through, I find a colorfully patterned N95 mask in bright reds and blues. It has a bohemian mandala design; I carefully fold and tuck it in the front pocket of my jeans, as I'm sure I'll find a use for it, even though they're now optional. Although the mandates have let up, at least this one can still be used when the next virus hits. It's unique and artsy. Glad I found it.

Last night Denny was in his office on another marathon video call with Mark. It lasted for an hour and a half. When he climbed into bed later, Denny mentioned the class again, saying we should check it out. Yes, "we"—meaning me too. I've no clue why I'm now included. He mumbled that if it made Mark change so drastically, it must be good. I sleepily agreed.

However, tonight during our fight about my horrible imperfections, Denny dared to bring up Mark's invitation. He sassily said the event involves Christianity. Umm. Well, my husband should know that's not a fair way to fight.

Denny's not an alcoholic; he—we—both drink beer, wine, and hard drinks but not to excess, so hopefully, the class won't be about addictions. And to prove how open-minded and thoughtful I am (I, the one deemed a sinner who is inconsiderate of others), I'll sit through a one-hour meeting for my husband's sake and keep my opinions to myself, only because I agreed to go. I can show Denny I'm receptive and thoughtful of others' views and beliefs, even if they differ from mine. See, I'm not like Amy.

Oh, well. The sacrifices and compromises we make to maintain relationships.

Back to my problem at hand.

I could tell you about many women I know who have had an abortion and seem to do perfectly fine in getting on with their lives. Take Zoey, for instance, who lives in our complex. Although I've known her for only six months, we hit it off from the start. I consider her my best friend. Well, maybe my only *true* friend.

She's seven years older than I am; we get along well because we both aspire to the same professional model. She's a hardcore career woman who happened to get pregnant twice but felt it wasn't the time for her to be a mother. The first guy was a college sweetheart, and she knew she didn't want to be married or tied down to a child. They agreed it would be best to terminate the baby, and within a half year, the relationship dissolved. Her second time involved a married man who never found out about it; their relationship lasted only a couple of months because he decided to stay with his wife. Who would want to have to deal with that issue? Would you want a child who has no father figure around? Rochelle is dealing with that. No thanks.

Being a hoity-toity, well-paid financial wizard in the banking industry, Zoey knows what she wants and gets it. She doesn't seem to have any problems being pro-choice; at least she's never mentioned that her past actions bother her or that she wishes she'd done things differently.

I know a couple of other girls who decided to abort, and both act as if they survived. Even Jeremy, the coworker I mentioned earlier, got a gal pregnant in college, but they didn't want to keep the baby. The relationship had ended before they found out, but he still paid for half of the procedure and took her to the clinic. They moved on, never to see each other again. Do you wonder if either one of them thinks about it all these years later? Are there any negative ripple effects?

Hmm. What's your take? You may think things have changed since *Roe v. Wade* was overturned at the federal level, but I live in California, which is still pro-choice, so I'm not too concerned about seeking and getting quality healthcare in handling the problem. But if I lived in the Midwest, that would be an entirely different issue.

What would you do if you were in my shoes? And don't give me that pat line, "I'd never be in your shoes," as you never know until it happens to you.

You might tell me to ask my parents.

That's certainly not going to happen.

Mom would smother me with affirmations to make my own decision; Daddy would say, "Whatever you want, Cupcake," but be stand-offish and distant. Probably it would cause a wedge between them, and they would argue. The last thing I want is the two of them fighting.

And my sister? If Silvia knew I was even contemplating getting rid of this baby, she'd un-sister me and never speak to me again.

Also, I'd feel the shame of not matching up to the perfect person my parents, sister, and others think I am. I have my dignity and pride. It would make me look like I'm not in control. I'm always logical, and I'm always in control, even if I have to pretend to be. Always.

I could keep an abortion a secret from everyone, including Denny, my entire life. Would you keep silent about it if you had one? No one could or would know.

In a last-ditch effort, I glance over at my cell phone on the island counter and think about Zoey again. She might be able to tell me if she had any problems or concerns. I quickly pick up the device and send a short text message to her: *Call me when you can, girl. Need your expertise.*

She should be able to help me get through this strange phase. She can tell me if the procedure is painful and what to expect.

After contemplating, more like arguing all sides I can think of, I've made up my mind. The internal debate is over.

You notice me holding out my hands, staring at my manicured fingernails.

See my wedding ring Denny designed with a lovely marquise diamond on white gold? Silver thumb ring on the same hand? Young, vibrant hands? Determined hands.

That's it. I've decided.

Pleased that I've made a decision and moved a couple of items out of the junk drawer as well, I close the messy box with ease and stretch my hands above my head. I feel a sense of determination.

Like the now-shut drawer, my problem needs closure, too.

I'll find a local clinic after my parents leave town; I'll get it handled and over with then.

Done.

No more discussion.

No more God-talk either.

And for that matter, it's time to keep Denny away from Mark and his religion, meeting or no meeting.

~ Girls ~

Enough.

Please, no more thinking or psychology. Don't get me started and don't question me. I'm done.

No more analyzing.

No more comparing.

The decision stands as is.

Back to the real world.

Sarah is in control.

I must stop wasting time. The baking pan has soaked long enough in the sink. Back to something simple like getting burnt cheese off a stubborn dish. Next time I'll remember to spray a heavy dose of Pam on the sides of the pan too.

The girls continue to swing back and forth on the swing set, back and forth. Based on the gently swaying leaves of a nearby maple tree, there is a light breeze.

Giggling.

Swinging back and forth.

Laughing.

They seem so carefree.

I study them further as I lift the sink's plug and let the lukewarm water run out. I've noticed both girls in the building's compound a couple of times. Both Latinas have dark brown hair. The older one looks about eight years old. Darling. The other has shorter, wavy hair and looks related, but a few years younger. Cute kids with matching dimples when they smile. One is wearing a red polka-dot dress that reminds me of when Silvia and I used to watch those old Shirley Temple movies when we stayed home sick from school. I don't know who the girls' parents are. The children are enjoying themselves. They look safe, with no one else in view or bothering them.

The older girl is tilting her head back as far as she can, looking upward as she jets her feet outward on the upswing, like she's flying upside down.

On the windowsill sits Denny's gift of white tulips for our anniversary last week. In my grandmom's cherished crystal vase, they are looking a little droopy. I carefully water them and return the vase to its place of honor. I look back at the girls again, reminiscing how freeing swinging felt as a kid—a time when COVID didn't exist, and unwatched kids weren't abducted like sometimes they are nowadays. If I had a child and that happened, the fear would be unimaginable.

I bend down and open the cupboard below the sink. I move the dishwashing detergent to the side to retrieve a pot-scrubbing brush that sits in an old bowl at the back of the cabinet.

WHAT WAS THAT?

What an odd noise.

Not a yell or a scream, not a siren, not a horn blaring.

Like a shout.

A weird sound, a noise I've never heard in my life.

Did you hear it? A strange sound—a booming voice, maybe?

What do you think it could be? Have you ever heard anything like it?

A noise I can't describe. Like a word, but not. Several sounded syllables, you think? No. Short, noticeably short sounds, as if several are put together at once. Similar to music—a trumpet sound?

Encompassing everything, but not.

An eerie, weird sound. I hear and feel it inside my body.

What a peculiar noise.

Can't exactly figure it out. Can you?

Like a word, a shout, and a trumpet—all three sounds at once.

Do you know what it is? Can you explain that sound or sounds? Surely you heard it, too. How would you describe it?

Unique.

Surreal.

I feel a sharp twinge in my gut.

I STAND BACK UP WITH the brush in my hand.

My eyes gravitate to the window again.

The two little girls are gone.

Only two swings are swaying.

Empty.

How weird.

Where did the girls go?

Did you see them leave?

Did they jump off the swing and run over to another section of the complex? Run that fast, in the time it took me to duck down and come back up? No way. I peer down the sidewalk to the right. Look to the left. Nothing. No one. Did our security camera by the front door catch something?

No child or adult can move that fast.

I notice a few articles of clothing flittering away near the swings, moving out of my view.

Looks like a dress, maybe some underwear.

Wasn't one of the girls wearing that red polka-dotted outfit?

My eyes search the lawn for more clothing. There, by the jungle gym, another piece. A shirt.

I scan back to the swings, still moving back and forth, empty. Not as hard as before, tapering down, slower and slower.

After putting the brush down in the sink, I move the vase of flowers farther over to the right. I try to look past the playground to an access street and empty field, but see no movement, no cars, no people.

Haphazardly strewn in the sand are two pairs of shoes. A sock or two here and there, tossed about randomly.

Weird.

Dennis? I want to say his name aloud, but something stops me.

I hear a dog barking in the distance.

Off to the right through the window, I see a lady who's down the sidewalk, in full view of the playground, running toward it, screaming.

"Carmen! Alesha! Where are you?" she wails in a horror-filled tone as her hands hold her cheeks in shock.

Where are they?
Where did they go?
I'm at a loss for words.
Do you see them anywhere?

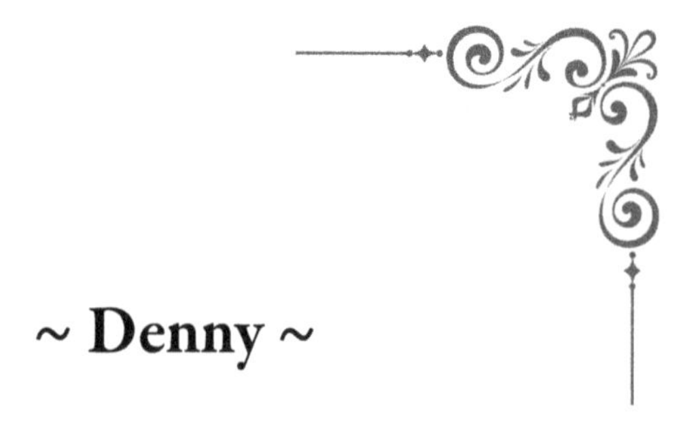

~ Denny ~

"Denny!" I scream frantically.

No answer.

"Denny?"

No answer.

"Den!"

Typical. When I need him the most, he doesn't answer. Probably wearing those over-priced, noise-canceling headphones so can't hear a mouse peep. You can hear me, but my husband is oblivious to my yelling.

"Alexa," I press the access button on the refrigerator, hoping she'll calm my nerves. "What just happened?"

"Um. I don't know ...," she replies.

"Alexa—stop!" I never can ask the right question in the right way for these robotic electronics to answer me correctly.

I try again. "Alexa, what was that strange sound I heard seconds ago?"

"According to what I found on the Internet, the sound heard sixteen seconds ago is undetermined." Great, a non-answer. Ugh. This is why I don't like talking aloud to things made of plastic and metal.

I must tell Denny about the girls. I want to ask him if he heard that strange sound or happened to look down from the office window to the playground. Can he check the security camera for replays? What's his take on this? Where is he, and why hasn't he come out of his office? No way could he not have heard that sound. What's he doing?

Do you have any clue what's happening? Are you as baffled as I am?

I run toward the staircase and start up the first two steps, but something stops me.

A cramp, a pain in my abdomen.

A sharp throb, as if a pointed, serrated knife is jammed into the lower right side of my abdomen.

Barefoot, I pivot on the stairs, holding onto the wood banister, and step back onto the floor. Balancing myself along the wall to the downstairs bathroom, I try not to stumble or fall.

Sharp, sharp pain.

I stop and take a shallow breath.

"Denny?" I cry but not as loud.

I'm scared. What do I tell him? What will I say? Will he have to know that I'm pregnant? Will he get mad that I didn't tell him? How should I phrase it? Should I pretend I'm full of joy about it? What should I do? What's this incredible pain? Do you know what's happening to me?

I trip into the bathroom, accidentally hitting both the fan and light switches at the same time. Cussing to the nonstop swirling noise, I slam the door closed behind me. We must fix that fan; there's something wrong with it being so loud as it rhythmically clangs.

Repeating my recent life-altering experience, I unzip my jeans and sit down on the toilet seat again.

Blood rushes out and colors the water.

I check to see how much blood—not too much, but enough—plenty. Do you think that I ...?

The pang within me instantly subsides. Now it appears that I have menstrual cramps.

Hmm, I ponder. Could I be having my period?

Maybe the fever I had last month messed up my cycle. That, or I have internal bleeding; maybe I lost the baby. Perhaps this bleeding *was* the baby; maybe it couldn't live in my womb. Do I have something wrong with me, a bad tube or ovary, scarred uterus, or cancer that's causing this blood? My mind races through possible death-threatening issues within seconds.

Do you do that when you're frightened? Within nanoseconds, you think up the most unbelievable situations imaginable, although they're most likely impossible to happen. Hate when I do that, but here I'm doing it again.

Or I must not be pregnant.

Yeah, do you think so?

I'll bleed a little, and that'll be all. Everything will be fine; I know it. Either way, I'm in control.

Guess I should call Zoey and make sure everything is right with me; she knows what to expect.

I open a nearby cabinet, retrieve a tampon, and grab a bottle of Motrin for the pain.

Woah.

A relief encompasses me as I clean myself up and wash my hands.

I'm not pregnant. I can't be pregnant now. There's too much blood.

There must be no baby. Maybe there never was a baby, right?

A misreading on the stick. A false alarm.

All that fretting was a waste of time.

I'm okay.

See, everything is back to normal. Good.

I pop two capsules in my mouth and cup my hand to the running water from the faucet to capture enough water to down them.

Recalling how I looked at myself in the mirror minutes ago, I determinedly inspect my reflection with triumph.

I'm not pregnant. I'm fine.

All is back to normal.

Nothing to worry about except for getting the obnoxious-sounding vent in the ceiling above me fixed.

With my hands damp from the water, I pat my cheeks to restore their color. I feel refreshed. I feel anew. Confident and determined. I stare at myself and repeat aloud, over and over, the words I've often said for many years—my mantra: "I'm in control. Sarah, you're in control."

I'm relieved. I've had enough excitement for one day.

I'm sorry I put you through that, but I bet we're both glad it's over.

On to the next topic: What's the deal with that strange sound, and what about those two little girls? Where did they go? What was with their clothing being sprawled all over the playground and grass?

Do you know if that odd sound was important, or was it a fluke?

You had to hear it, so does that mean Denny did, too?

~ Noises ~

Still cramping, I hit the blaring ceiling fan and light switches off and exit the bathroom again. I'm resolved to forget the last half hour. Not preggo, what a relief.

As I open the bathroom door, I yell, "Denny?"

Outside noises loudly compete with my scream.

Cries from a mother. That lady who was calling for her two girls must be frantic. The sound of her voice wailing is interminable. She must be right outside on the walkway by our patio's gate. It sounds like she and a man are arguing. Something about her accusing him of taking her adorable kids. She laments that they were right there on the swings, and now there's no trace of them. I can't and don't want to hear her shrieking. Can you hear her? Is it driving you crazy, too? The odious woman is relentless.

"Denny?" I holler upstairs once again, trying to outmatch her din. What a flake he is. Can't he hear all these noises? Can you believe him sometimes? He's pulled stunts like this before when we've argued. He ignores me or doesn't speak to me for hours. Drives me crazy. It's as if he's not here. I've no problem getting your attention, but I can't get his right now.

Mixing with the mother's mournful wails is crying from the unit next to ours. Sounds like our next-door neighbor

Adam's voice crying, "No, Poppa, no. Not now. No." Adam's a middle-aged bachelor, and his dear eighty-year-old father lives with him. Such a nice old-timer who's polite and kind. The first time I met him, he gave me a silver one-dollar coin, remarking he does it for everyone who crosses his path. Rambled something about "render unto Caesar the things that are Caesar's."

Occasionally, the son intermingles foul language with his rant, repeating the words "no" and "Poppa." Why would Adam use profanity around his father? He's never sworn like that before when we hear any loud conversations between the thinly plastered walls.

Car alarms are going off. I run to the living room bay window, stand on my tiptoes, and gaze over my flowers to the far right where there's a partial view of a common parking lot that can be seen between our patio's fence and the walkway to our front door. I notice the Alexa unit has an orange glow, meaning there's a notification.

"Alexa, what's my notification?" I hope she answers me this time.

"I'm sorry, but we're having technical difficulties."

Enough already with these worthless electronics!

After yanking the cordless device off its stand, I hurl it against the fireplace. It bounces off the brick tiles and cracks, its pieces clattering on the hearth.

I go back to looking outside; about a half dozen residents are standing next to three cars in the parking lot. Looks like a simple car accident. A white Toyota Prius has crashed into a beat-up green Volvo station wagon, yet there's a look of bewilderment by those standing near a third vehicle. It looks like at least two insurance companies will be raising their drivers' rates the second the claims get filed.

Past them at the far end of the lot is a solo black Dodge SUV with all-black tinted windows, blocking the entrance, presumably dead in its tracks. Nobody's hanging around it. What's the deal?

I hear emergency sirens, maybe police or fire trucks, in the distance. Sounds like several of them going in different directions. The multiple sirens remind me of Daddy telling me about the 1950s and 60s civil-alert drills where he had to crawl under his desk during school. Blindly obeying, he and other students thought hiding under a pathetic metal structure would save them from a nuclear blast. This isn't anything like that or the ongoing terrorist bombing alerts or sniper lockdowns at schools or stores. Although I was a child, I remember our country being attacked; I can't imagine experiencing 9/11 again, or any other bombing since then. I thought we're safer nowadays; it's overseas in those funky Middle Eastern countries where there are continual conflicts. Often, it's Israel, not us, that has been the problem. Yes, the world has changed drastically in the last twenty-plus years, with viruses, skyrocketing inflation, empty store shelves, and supply-chain disruptions, but we're still here and functioning.

My, what happened when I was in the bathroom for mere minutes?

What's your take on this? Are you as bemused as I am?

I scan the grassy parkway area next to the parking lot and focus, observing the view with a journalistic eye. An unattended lawnmower is stopped at the end of a straight line of grass while a trail of clothing neatly rests behind it. Three teenagers in T-shirts and jeans stand ten feet away on a sidewalk, appearing to be in a conversation. The one I've seen before with tattoos inked on both his arms bounces a basketball, head down, not looking at the other two talking. Suddenly, a scantily dressed teenage girl with short shorts comes running up to the three, pulling on the basketball guy's arm frantically. She must want him to go with her. Her body language conveys she's distraught; she keeps pawing him.

The front of our townhouse faces another two-story building with single-bedroom units. It has an exterior stairway, and I see white smoke pouring out of an upper unit. Two men with hand-held fire extinguishers stand on the stairs and top landing. One is wearing only boxer shorts while the other is in a gray suit with a blue tie. A teen in a T-shirt and jeans comes out of the smoky condo, coughing. He looks frightened as the two men grab him and help him down the stairs. He throws up in the ajuga ground cover next to the walkway. He remains bent over, hands firmly on both knees, possibly waiting for the next round of nausea.

What's going on, and what's next? It seems like the entire area around me is falling apart in seconds. Do you see this? What do you think?

"Denny!"

No response.

My anger toward that man is growing. Well, I can keep on playing his game if he's still mad at me. Remember, I aim to win. Always. He needs to grow up, let me know what's going on, and be the one to break the silence first, not me.

Remain calm and collected, Sarah. There's a logical explanation for this weirdness.

Then I hear a motoring sound, sputtering and choking, getting louder and louder. It sounds like it's coming from above the townhouse. I stretch my neck and look upward through the bay window, outside, between two of the buildings, above the unit that had been spewing out white smoke.

There—a plane, an extremely low-flying plane.

The aircraft looks like a Boeing 737, the mid-size type that holds over a hundred-and-fifty people. It has one engine under each wing and is veering off to the left of the housing units.

I have no time to look at the few bystanders or the barfer's reactions. Their silhouettes are in my vision; they are stick figures, motionless in my mind. My eyes are concentrating on the plane. The plane passes the groups of cookie-cutter townhouses slowly, tipping on its side with one of the wings barely grazing the roof of the building across from us. That close!

The roar is horrendous; the windows are rattling.

I see no flames, no smoke. Only a plane almost sideways in the sky and way too close to the buildings.

Screeching engine noises fill my home. The floor is shaking below my feet.

I run to the kitchen to look out the window above the sink as the plane continues to bank left.

"Denny!" I helplessly yell over the constant noise and vibration.

A thunderous rumble fills the sky as the plane passes by my view. The aircraft tilts farther on its side; I'm guessing it's thirty feet above the playground. The empty swings bow at the rush of wind and passing of the jet. No smoke. No fire.

The window shakes and rattles. I feel the floor tremble as I hold on to the counter and stretch myself toward the windowpane, trying not to knock over the vase that I had moved over on the sill.

My eyes don't leave the scene as the plane passes, as if in slow motion.

It's barely in my sight now, headed for the field on my far left. Toward the desolate football-field-sized terrain that caught fire about years ago during the Santa Ana winds that burned down hundreds of nearby homes. Thankfully, the wind switched directions and spared our complex. Now the field has wild orange and yellow California poppies and overgrown weeds.

I press my cheek to the window glass, straining to watch the plane's final descent.

Bam!

An astronomically loud thud occurs.

The sound is so shocking it startles me; the vase starts to tip into the sink from me elbowing it. I catch it in time, spilling water on my hands and into the still-dirty lasagna pan, yet all the vase's flowers stay intact.

When the plane hits the ground with a tumultuous boom, only a part of its tail section can be seen from my window. At once, a bright red and yellow fireball shoots a couple of hundred feet upward into the cloudless blue sky. Black smoke billows out of the aircraft's tail.

Without flinching, I grasp my smartphone from the island top, grab a towel with my wet hand, and hit the number "4" button with a cloth-covered finger. My work number.

I go back to the window to try to examine the carnage in the field.

Are you still here? Are you seeing this? Can you believe it?

"Valley News," Carl states in a short and gruff voice that I recognize instantly, but that sounds highly tensed and strained. My boss. Why is he answering the phone when he has an entire staff at his disposal?

"Carl, Sarah here. Listen, I may have something hot. A plane grazed past my kitchen window and crashed in a field by the complex. I'm unsure if hit the nearby church or not." I say the words fast and succinctly, determined to state my case. "I have my gear, so I'm going to run over for photos. Can you leave space for a picture or video? High-priority Internet and print footage."

He doesn't seem to be listening to me. Here I practically have a plane fall out of the sky right on top of me and have the perfect opportunity for capturing "the Big Photo" that can go global, and he's not excited.

As I speak on the phone, I quickly go to my photo bag by the front door and pick up my digital video camera. Denny got it for me three birthdays ago. One good thing about his job is he can get any consumer electronic gadget at or below wholesale cost. My beloved Nikon D4 Digital SLR camera has 16.2 megapixels and a CMOS sensor with FX-format and image processor. I know that means nothing to you, and you don't give a hoot. There's probably a camera that's more up to date for professional applications with more doodads, but this camera rocks. It's an excellent device, my prized possession. I check the zoom and make sure I've got enough space on the digital card for tons of award-winning photos; its worn leather strap wraps around my neck. This is going to get attention; I know it. You watch.

Intuitively other thoughts must be occupying Carl's attention, but he interrupts me. "Things are freaking out everywhere," he says, "and I've sent everyone out in the field. The world has gone upside-down. Major things are happening spontaneously, things I've never seen in my life. Strange things.

"Go, Sar. The entire flipped-out world is going whack. The world is a madhouse. Too much is going on at one time."

I answer, confused. "Okay." He tells me to be safe and that he has no promises, then ends the call.

Perturbed about his aloofness, I tuck my phone in the back pocket of my jeans. I pull on my neon yellow press vest complete with a clip-on credentials badge and swing my gear bag over my shoulder.

Well, I'll show Carl. I'll give him the best, incredible video of a plane crash he's ever seen. This will make me well-known. Sarah Colton has arrived once again, and you're with me to see it happen.

Holding onto the entry area's table for balance, I slip my bare feet into the black clogs I ritualistically leave under the stand, and I'm ready to go, fully loaded. I scream once more up the stairs, "Denny!"

Where is that man, and how could he not have heard that plane crash? What a dolt.

Hmm. Maybe he left the house when I was in the bathroom with that silly pregnancy issue. Could be.

You didn't see him go, did you?

If he left, he could've at least knocked on the door and told me.

I notice that his keys and smartphone remain untouched on the entrance table. With a shaky hand, I pull out a pen from the side pocket of my gear bag and scribble a quick note on the back of an opened envelope from the Humane Society asking for a donation:

D ~
Where R U? At plane 4 pics.
Luv,
~ S

AS I COVER DENNY'S cell phone with my note, I stop for a second and bitingly repeat what Amy blared out about her God tonight, "... and He shall direct thy paths." Right. Well, I'm directing my paths right over to that plane and taking pictures so I can be famous. I'm in control.

I open the front door and step out into a strange world of uncertainty.

~ Plane ~

After pulling the front door closed, I rush down the sidewalk of our enclosed patio, careful not to stumble over the potted Abracadabra rose Amy gave us. I love a flower that changes color every season, and it needs water badly, but who am I to have time to be a gardener, especially when I can get the picture of the year? As I pass the security camera focused on the front door, I file a mental note to have Denny check it later. I sprint past the gate and down the walkway, pass the community mailboxes, and turn left toward the playground.

My heart is pounding; I'm thankful I only have minor cramping, and I know the Motrin will be kicking in soon. My mind is racing. This could be "the photo."

Are you keeping up with me? I don't know what shape you're in health-wise, but step it up, as we must get to the scene before anyone else.

My last climbing-the-corporate-ladder-in-one-fell-swoop was when the governor's son got shot. It was a sheer accident that I was in the convenience store at that exact time, buying a bottle of cabernet. I had mistakenly carried my camera bag into the store instead of my over-the-shoulder purse. Boy, what a smart mistake I made.

I was at the back of the store and headed to the checkout counter, wine in hand, but I had noticed one of my pant legs folded up on its hem, so I bent down to straighten it out with my other hand. In doing so, I didn't immediately notice the trouble unfolding in front of me.

Two robbers were holding the governor's son at gunpoint in the middle of the chip aisle. One was holding the kid's arm while the other was facing him. From where I was standing, I had a full view of the three, as I was at the far-end kiosk of the same aisle but out of view of the creep holding the gun. Hovering near the row of Doritos, I slowly slipped the beat-up Nikon that Daddy had given me for my eighteenth birthday out of the bag, nonchalantly held it out six inches from my hip, and pressed the button once without looking through its viewfinder.

One click—a click loud enough that it caught the gunman's peripheral attention as he pulled the trigger. Unfortunately, the weapon went off, and the bullet hit the poor boy on the side of the head. Oh, blood went everywhere. At that second, I had no clue what kind of photo I got, but I remember being scared to death when the shooter looked in my direction.

As the robber holding the kid saw his partner shoot, he hollered for them to split before the cops arrived. By then, the bloody boy was on the floor, not moving, while the deep red puddle under his head rapidly expanded. I had sunk to the floor in shock, waiting for the assailant to whip around the corner and put a bullet in my brain. The last thing I was thinking about was what my photograph showed. Once I knew the thugs had fled, I ran to the unconscious boy's side and held him as I sobbed, begging for someone to help.

Sure enough, when the nightmare was over, right on my camera was the tell-all photograph of the two robbers' faces—in plain view with the gun firing, the exact second of the killing! Police were ecstatic that they could identify and later arrest the crooks so easily. My photo made front-page news, and the syndicate bought it. I have at least a dozen printed copies of the various news sources and a list of the many websites that showed it online. Cable networks included it as their headline news of the day. Got a nice, nickel-framed copy of it at my office workstation. The governor called the news, talked to Carl, and wrote me a thoughtful and tender letter plus later sent a case of the wine I was trying to buy. Although his son had been holding on to life while he had been in my lap, he died three days later, never having regained consciousness.

Have you been through anything like that? It's traumatic and unexplainable. The experience left me shaken and withdrawn when I realized that I may have caused the gun to go off by taking the photo, or that I could've been shot, too, by those drug-crazed hoodlums. I took a week off work and started going to counseling for post-traumatic stress. It's strange seeing someone getting shot in the head and dying as I held him close. After several months of therapy, the hardest thing for me to do was to throw out my blood-stained pants, shirt, jacket, and shoes, as if keeping them would have brought the kid back to life.

But what happens happens.

My sessions also taught me about overcoming guilt and staying calm during a crisis by putting all feelings, good or bad, on the back burner until later. I learned that logic was my friend.

The gov's son's time was up, and mine was not.

And no, it didn't change my thinking about an afterlife in Heaven or Hell like others do. Nor did it make me grasp onto God from an out-of-body incident. I moved on, thanks to the shrink I went to who said my healing was inside me, and I can accept and change how I perceive my experiences, good or bad. I cured myself. That's when I realized I was in control, not anyone or any Superior Being. Me and only me.

Do I need to reiterate? Yes, I was and am in control. And you're in control of yourself; don't let anyone try to tell you differently. Do yourself a favor and ignore them if they pull that talk on you.

This time, I won't let that wave of emotion latch onto me. I'll be an observer, not a participant. I'm there to take videos and pics for a story, nothing more. No involvement, no reaction.

With my adrenaline soaring, I'm determined to overcome my nervous panic. I force myself to accept that the funny feeling in my stomach is only cramping, nothing else ... including a growing baby.

I run past the playground and swing set, not stopping to look at or pick up those girls' articles of clothing. Hmm. Did you notice them, too, and are you wondering what happened?

The plane or remains of its scattered parts are clearly in my vision, as though it's taking up the full screen of a movie theater. One other person is running to the crash site. Several people stand frozen in awe in the access street watching the wreckage, doing nothing.

Dark clouds of smoke billow and surge upward to the evening sky from parts of the broken metal ship. I stop in my tracks. My camera focuses automatically, and I pan the area with the video finder, scanning back and forth, trying not to wobble and shake as I keep my finger on the "On" button.

The plane is separated into several sections: The back part of the fuselage sprawls on the dry ground a hundred feet directly in front of me; the front part, including the cockpit and both separated wings, is on fire at the far-left end of the field, less than thirty yards from the First Baptist Church. The broken tail, with its marred airline logo, rests to the right near an arterial street, standing like a monumental tombstone pointing to the sky, to an unknown god. Ironically, I notice the occasional orange and yellow poppies blowing casually in the wind around the carnage, as if not paying attention to the tragedy that surrounds them.

Help me here. Remind me to focus, pan out the camera, and concentrate on holding it still. Tell me to stay in control; tell me not to get involved, to stay restrained. Sagacity must rule.

I pass the grass area designated for dog-walking, not concerned if I step in any unintentionally or intentionally left excrement. I jump off the sidewalk curb and travel across the complex's access road, making sure I don't trip over the speed bump that needs a new coat of yellow paint.

On the outer apron of the street rests an abandoned bicycle on its side. It looks like one of those top-of-the-line models with all the special gears and gadgets as its chrome sparkles in the setting sun. A pair of men's white athletic shoes with their laces tied, white socks, and black running shorts are tossed nearby. A neon green shirt is splayed across one wheel's spokes, while a black bike helmet with earbuds hanging from it is spotted in the nearby weeds. The owner must be at the crash site. Why did he leave without some of his clothes and shoes?

I wish you'd tell me repeatedly to focus, zoom in, and hold the camera still, Sarah. I must be at peace. Relax. I inhale and exhale through my nose as slowly as I can. I must be calm, so there's no shakiness in the video.

Is your blood pressure rising like mine? Can you help relax me—tell me something, anything to ease this growing panic?

Now I am about twenty feet from the back half of the fuselage.

Stop, focus, zoom, pan left, and pan right. Slowly, slowly. No shake.

Bent metal pieces, parts of torn airline seats, tattered clothing, and human debris lie scattered at my feet. I'm afraid to move, to step forward or on something or on someone's body part.

As I observe the destruction in my viewfinder, the scene sears into my mind forever. Focus, focus, Sarah. Stay calm and collected. This time I open my mouth and take a breath. I know that's a small breath. Try again. Breathe. Don't get involved. Please, you help me concentrate; please help me be calm.

Panning the camera, I hear screams. Not the screams you hear on a breath-crushing roller coaster, but more the kind that knows death is approaching and inevitable. I could never imagine or explain this scene of such horrendousness. I want to put words to the splattered blood, the twisted metal, the acrid smell of burning flesh, and the unworldly screams, or to how cruelly the plane engulfs its victims, but I can't mouth them. I know no words, do you? I want to plug my ears—the cries are horrific. My mouth feels full of cotton; my eyes are watery from smoke, and my legs want to buckle. I'm in a fight-or-flight situation; I must fight. I must stay in control.

Carefully, I step over a puddle of blood oozing from a hot pink sock and matching Nike tennis shoe tied onto a foot and ankle minus its body. Red blood is oozing onto the pretty sock from the foot inside the shoe as it remains unmovable on its side.

I'd tell you not to look, but you can't miss seeing the death surrounding me. I want to simply do my job.

Focus on the mundane.

The shattered face plate of a man's Fitbit with an all-black band blinks its racked-up digits in the nightmare, never to register another step.

A tall dandelion weed flutters with a part of someone's head—oh, several strands of long gray hair with red chunks of scalp—dangling off the leaves. Stop, don't look, move on, Sarah.

A tan cardboard cup sits upright, a stir stick still in place and the remains of cream-laced coffee still evident. A finger nearby with a fake neon lime green nail resides next to a partially weed-filled gopher hole. A pair of glasses, one lens cracked with blood splatters. A man's brown leather wallet, folded and unopened, resting on the airline's emergency insert card. And, by a partial leg, a smartphone facing down, its cover filled with sparkly rhinestones on a cyan-colored backing.

Stop looking, forget what you're seeing. Let the camera do the work, not me.

You notice my heart pumping each beat through my veins. My stomach is queasy, is yours? The palms of my hands are clammy. It seems like hours instead of seconds have passed.

Fixated on my viewfinder, I barely notice a man rushing past me. He's saying something about standing back; he has a small fire extinguisher, like those kept in the entry halls of our townhouse buildings. He's telling me he wants to get to the passengers, to see if any are alive or injured.

I hear him, yet he sounds far away, in a long, dismal tunnel from a world parallel to ours.

Looking up, away from the viewfinder to the side of the field opposite the church, I see a solo fire truck entering its parking lot with its lights flashing and three firefighters hurrying to unload equipment. Near what's left of the front half of the fuselage and wings, the crew has set up hoses and is shooting water into the blaze. It's a good thing the vicious, fire-seeking Santa Ana winds aren't raging through the Valley today.

As fast as the defining screams started, they instantly hush. No more yelling can be heard; all is silent except for the fires prodding and torturing the man-made metal at the crash scene.

I bravely take the next several steps and follow the man who ran past me. Don't look down, Sarah—don't look at those things on the ground, those items that breed everlasting nightmares. Look straight ahead at the plane.

Control yourself.

Try to take another breath.

Do you see this carnage too? Unbelievable. Unfathomable.

The muscular man is positioning his head into the ripped-opened area of what remains of the back half of the fuselage. He's putting out a small fire to the right of the opening with the bright red canister. Amazingly, this portion of the plane is not engulfed by flame—maybe because the fuel-stored wings tore off and are far enough away from what's left here.

I stand five feet behind him.

Focus, pan.

Slow, steady.

Exhale calmly.

My camera zooms past the large man into the destroyed craft. I unemotionally scan past parts of bodies, human beings, trying not to glance at their faces and features, but it's hard and impossible to avoid.

As the man sprays carbon dioxide and extinguishes the fire in the plane's opening, a body is discovered. Next to it is another one; both are burned to the point that their sex is indeterminable. Yet across the aisle is a seemingly unscathed male in his mid-forties: bald with glasses, paunch hanging over his fastened seat belt, blue button-up-the-front shirt, and dark slacks. He sits as though he's dozed off; I'm grateful there's no look of panic or fear on his face. I blink and move the camera to the next victim. Guessing from the color of her hair, a woman in her sixties is flopped over, hugging a cushion or pillow. Thankfully, I can't see her face. A thin woman with one leg twisted in an unnatural direction wears a face mask; her thick, black-rimmed glasses are askew on her nose. Her head is hanging limply on her chest; she's dead. A man with a noticeable alchemy eye tattoo on his neck and gauges in both earlobes is in his seat, eyes closed while his head is tilted backward. Dead.

It looks like no one is alive. The tomb of death is displayed in front of my camera, in front of me. In front of you.

The video continues to pan; I'm on autopilot, watching a movie on a tiny screen that I hold in my hand instead of being here, in the flesh, directly in front of me. Maybe I'm feeling like you are—here to only see and hear, but not to participate or interact. I know I'm alive, but I'm deeply aware that those around me are not.

My arms tingle and go weak for a second, forcing me to drop my camera on its shoulder strap, thudding against my breastplate as if it refuses to view more tragedy and horror. I look down at the mechanical object barely moving on my chest, hoping it's not as broken as my heart feels.

The automatic videotaping continues, homed in on the floor of the plane.

There—under the seat by the aisle on the right side—it shows a black briefcase that's half-open with papers blowing and flapping around.

Leaving the camera at my chest level but able to turn the front knob and view the screen, I zoom in further into the broken aircraft, under the seat, three rows back, and concentrate on the movement of the papers.

Look at something not human, Sarah. Something inactive, not alive. Never alive. Stay in control. Try breathing through the nose again; you know it calms you down. Be levelheaded.

A pure white sock. A gold bracelet. An airline ticket. Inanimate objects only.

Torn seat cover. Empty pretzel bag. Harlequin romance novel with its pages flipping one way and then the opposite direction. Several keys on a Seattle Mariners' keychain. An airline napkin with something scribbled on it. A capped gel pen.

Something arouses my interest.

Under a seat on the floor is an unopened candy bar jammed between the foot railings of the chair—a Trader Joe's dark chocolate bar—the kind Denny always buys for me. It's one of my favorites.

When I zoom in for a closer look, I overshoot and see beyond the treat and between the row of seats.

Oh, a hand! An outstretched hand, fully open, its palm facing outward toward the opening of the fuselage. All five fingers intact, no burnt skin, no marring of the palm or wrist.

I pause on the scene, taking a still shot of the unmoving hand. Then I let the video capture the humanity of the hand hanging down, hoping at any second, it'll grab the candy bar or give the okay sign with its first finger and thumb, and all will be well in the world.

Then it happens.

The hand moves!

Did you see that? Wow! I know you saw it too; I'm not fantasizing.

The first finger wavers a little at the first joint, then motions as though it's calling for a cab or wanting to call something to my attention. The connected fingers join in, pumping in and out slowly into the palm.

The hand is awake—the hand is alive!

~ Boy ~

I scream at once to the man with the fire extinguisher, "Over there, someone is alive!"

He turns and looks at me with amazement. The horror reflected in his bloodshot eyes evolves into a flicker of hope.

I point. "Left side, fourth row!"

The man tosses me the extinguisher as he climbs into the aircraft. As I grab the canister, I release my hands on my beloved camera, allowing it to yo-yo back and forth freely on its strap as it continues to document the indescribable scene.

There are no flames left inside the plane as the man carefully swings his leg up about two feet into the nightmarish hole. He grabs onto part of the bald man's armrest and pulls himself inside.

I step closer now, close enough to be able to reach out and touch the ghastly wreck.

The man moves cautiously down the aisle past three rows of bodies, all noticeably dead by their appearance of lifeless faces or twisted body parts. I try ignoring them as much as possible and suggest you do the same. He squats down behind the next row so I can't see what he's doing.

"Here, yes!" he calls out loudly as his head bobs up and down. "A kid is alive!"

I can't see what's happening, can you? I presume the man is helping the person sit up as the hand under the seat has disappeared from my vantage point.

Without thinking, I drop the fire extinguisher and pull my Nikon out in front of me. This time, however, I don't look at the viewfinder but let the camera run on its own—I keep my eyes glued to the man, hunched over in the aisle.

"You're okay; you're going to be okay," he repeats to the passenger.

I see the man haul a body up over his shoulder and retreat backward in my direction. The body looks like that of a young man, I'm guessing mid-teens, sporting short brown hair and an orange polo shirt with its collar flipped up, covering his neck. I can't see his face. His body is limp.

The boy starts to moan as the man approaches the opening, next to the bald man in the blue shirt.

Since both are now directly above me, you and I see the boy's face, which has a hint of facial hair. I guess he's fourteen or fifteen years old. He's waking up, and his eyelids are fluttering.

Unconsciously, I click the "Off" button on my camera and let it dangle against me.

The teen looks directly at me, his eyes empty at first, then opening wide in astonishment as he focuses on me.

Did you see the look on his face? Hard to forget, right?

As the boy continues to stare at me, I freeze in place, seeing so much anguish and fear conveyed by his eyes.

The man turns around and squats at the edge of the plane's floor. He asks me to help slip the boy off his shoulder, yet I don't respond. I can't move. I can't get past the boy's bewildered facial expression. I can't even lift my arms as they hang flimsily by my side. I don't do anything but stand there like a statue. I know you see my detached behavior, and I'm ashamed of it, but I still do not react.

The man gives me an exasperated look as he solely lifts and positions the kid in front of him. Without dropping the boy, the man slowly lowers him to the ground. On further inspection, I notice the guy must be a bodybuilder, as his hands are oversized, and his sweatshirt bulges at his biceps.

Again, I'm immobile, yet I detect the kid starting to thrash his arms and legs when he's a foot off the ground.

Although I know nothing about medicine, I visually inspect the boy's body. It looks lean but not skinny, about the same height as my five-foot-five-inch frame and weighing a little more than my one-hundred-and-twenty pounds. There appears to be neither blood gushing out of his orifices nor any twisted arms or legs. He looks unhurt.

As the teen's feet touch the dirt, his legs do not buckle or collapse; he stands but sways a little. The man keeps both hands on him, perhaps for his own support while leaping down from the plane.

My body finally catches up to my brain, and I act; I put my hand on the boy's arm and say, "Hold still; we're trying to help you," but he doesn't seem to hear.

Meanwhile, the man inspects the boy by walking around him and checking his hands, turning them over. Bearishly, the guy states in a commanding tone, "You look okay. This lady will take care of you," he tells him. "Lean on her."

Me? What am I supposed to do? I can't help this kid. I'm no medic. I didn't sign up for this job. I have no clue what to do here. I'm only a spectator taking a video. Not me! Do you have any advice?

I start to protest, but the man looks at me, too close to my face for comfort, and announces, "I'm gonna check the plane again to see if anyone else is in there."

He takes the boy's right arm and practically throws it over my shoulder, then turns back to the gaping hole that has become the plane's entrance. He jumps back in and continues up the aisle, searching for more survivors.

What should I do next? Maybe you can help me with him.

At least now the boy only has a glazed look in his eyes.

I ask him if he can walk to where we can get away from the awful scene behind us. I feel like I'm babbling. Can you tell if my actions and expressions are falling short of matching my words?

Then he does something odd. He moves his arm closer around me, protectively, pulling my face toward him with a bit of force. It makes me feel claustrophobic, being tugged close to his youthful body. He stares again at me, but not with that frightened look. I feel he is attempting to connect with me somehow, but I have no clue how to respond.

"Eddie's gone," he whispers hopelessly as our eyes meet.

Do you hear how distressing his words are? Do they haunt you like they do my heart?

I have no answer. I don't know how to act.

"It'll be fine," I say. "Hang in there. Let's get out of here," I add as though I'm talking to a school pal at recess, trying to share all the day's news before the bell rings. "Let's head over there," I point to the row of townhouses. "Maybe we can sit down on the curb?" I try to say anything to erase his look, his words.

As he and I stumble through the debris, body parts, dead weeds, and blooming poppies, he loosens his grip on me and supports himself more with each step. Neither of us looks down at the ground; we keep our gaze on the townhouse complex. I feel like we're running in a horse race and headed for the finish line, wearing blinders to keep us from any distractions.

When we are yards from the street, my cell phone rings in my pants pocket. I stop in my tracks without notifying the boy, almost causing both of us to stumble. I fish out the device, hoping it's Denny. Where did that man go? Looking at the caller ID, I see it's from my mom. She can wait for now. Nothing could be more traumatic than what I'm dealing with this minute, and the only other person I want to speak to right now is my husband.

Without answering, I numbly put the phone back.

While we step onto the worn asphalt, I notice the high-end bicycle is gone, as are the shoes and helmet. Only the athletic clothing remains, looking ransacked with both short pockets inverted. An open wallet lies in the middle of the street. There's no sign of the missing cyclist.

I nod to the boy that we can start walking again, and he obeys without speaking. Wordlessly,.we cross the access street, shuffling mindlessly over the speed bump. I help him sit down on the curb, shifting my camera bag off my shoulder and placing it between my legs. To avoid attracting attention from the now-growing crowd, I pull off my neon yellow vest with its press badge and jam it into my camera bag's side pocket.

We both take deep breaths and slowly exhale in unison as we sit in silence, reviewing the bad dream that, hopefully, is coming to completion in front of us.

The kid is alive. He'll be okay.

I'll be okay. I stayed in control. It's over now.

Don't you think I did well, considering all that's happened today? How are you? I know you're as tense as I am, but it's over. We got through it together. We're okay.

~ James ~

The firemen have put out the fires in the cockpit, wings, and tail, and are grouping around the fuselage where the man reentered. Meanwhile, I open my bag, pull out another video card, and exchange it for the used one in my camera. Handling the card like it's gold, I put it in a secured pouch and rest the camera back on my knees. The boy is watching what I'm doing but doesn't talk.

I pull out the viewfinder and focus one more time to capture the final moments of the grisly scene. I'm back to being an observer; I'm no longer a participant in a rescue operation. Back in my comfort zone as a composed journalist. My movements are systematic and routine.

Some of the tension has left my body; my heart no longer pounds in my chest. Saliva begins to return to my mouth. The medicine has helped calm my nerves and get me through the ordeal. The cramps have subsided. Overall, I feel normal and more like myself. Are you doing better, too?

The boy starts to sniffle, so he wipes his nose on one sleeve of his shirt several times without care. He takes the other sleeve and wipes both eyes with it. Black soot further stains the bright orange shirt with ash and debris.

I click the "On" button on the camera nonchalantly and ask, "So what's your name?" I continue to scan with my camera. "Mine is Sarah, Sarah Colton."

"James," he mumbles, "James Hixon."

"Nice to meet you, James—even though it's under these circumstances."

"You too, ma'am," he says, peering over my shoulder to see what I am doing with my camera.

Ma'am? I marvel. No kids these days use that kind of language, do they? Well, he's wearing Dockers, the polo shirt, and Nike high tops, so maybe he was brought up well. I bet he's a preppie at a private school. What's this boy's story? Where are his parents, and who is this Eddie person he mentioned while we walked through that revolting field? I'm afraid to ask, afraid of reminding him of whatever upsetting memory he has of the recent ordeal. Were his parents or siblings on the plane?

I try to implement the tricks my therapist taught me about dealing first-hand with someone dying and survivor guilt by keeping my voice soft and relaxed. Don't show any panic or excitement. Stay calm.

"How old are you, James?" I ask, trying to get him to come out of his horror-torn shell as I fiddle with my zoom lens and let the camera run, mainly for audio purposes.

"Fifteen and a half," he answers.

"Ah, got your driving permit then?"

"Yep, last week." He unties the laces on his left shoe, fiddles with them, removes a bur, and reties them.

Good, at least the kid is coherent and can function. I'd be scared if I had to again deal with someone who was severely injured or dying in my lap like the governor's son did. I'd have no clue what to do if he were screaming in pain right now, would you?

After scanning the video, I turn the camera off and gently place it in the bag. When I look up, a large golden retriever has made its way to James's side. The dog's leash is attached, but no owner follows. Immediately the canine licks the boy's face; he reciprocates by stroking the animal's head and scratching behind its ears. It's evident both find comfort in physical contact and affection. Then, as quickly as he came, the retriever wags his tail and continues his walk, dragging the leash behind.

By now, at least twenty to thirty people are milling around the perimeter of the field, gawking at the spread-out, death-filled debris. I see no appearance of Denny, only looky-loos wanting to get closer and see something disgusting. A cop car has arrived, and the policeman motions for everyone to stay back. No one is documenting the situation with high-end cameras; they're only using smartphones at best.

While James and I collect ourselves, I mention that I work for the *Valley News* and took pictures of the scene and plan to submit them. He replies he thinks it would be a cool job to have and asks a few innocuous questions about my camera, occupation, and if I had to go to college for it. He tells me he wants to be a writer. Surprisingly, the conversation is brief but almost normal.

Two people approach us from the wreck: One is the muscular man who rescued James, and the other is one of the firemen. They have slumped postures as they trudge among the growing crowd. Do you think they stepped up their gait when they saw us, determined to seek us out?

"Hi. Heard you survived; how are you doing, son?" asks the fireman, looking over the boy for any injuries. He's more than six feet tall and lanky. "Need assistance?"

The man who rescued James comes up behind the fireman, talkative to the point of making me nervous again. He introduces himself as Al King and tells James, "You're the only survivor, kid. Whatcha think of that? You're a hero. Any cuts or bruises? Looks like not even a scratch! Do you know I was the one who jumped in the plane to pull you out? If it weren't for me—well, this lady here saw you move around—but I was the one who hauled you out of that wreck. Miracle, a living miracle." He adds several inappropriate adjectives, probably part of his everyday speaking. I tuck away his name in my memory as I won't dare tell him who I am or what I do for a living. Does this guy rub you the wrong way, too? Hopefully, he's too preoccupied with himself to remember I had been wearing my press vest or notice my camera gear.

The fireman comments, apologetically, "Oh, we have no ambulances on the scene because of other incidents. Things are happening to the entire city. Hard to get one to come. Although this was a tragic accident with many lives lost, I'm glad you weren't seriously injured." I think, by the emotionless look on his face, the fireman may not want to discuss all the dead bodies and human parts strewn all over the field.

Muscleman Al interrupts, "So, want me to take you down to Holy Cross Hospital for a quick check-up? My truck is over in the parking lot." He points to the asphalt lot where the fender-bender occurred earlier. "It was amazing to see that plane come crashing down. What a racket it made. You did good, kid. Real good."

Based on his arms grasping tightly around his chest, James looks like he's ready to go in front of a firing squad or wants to crawl out of his body and be somewhere else. Wouldn't you want to be anywhere away from this man and his constant self-glorification?

Lo and behold. Look what I see.

A television van pulls up the private street and parks near a group of people. A little too late, boys and girls. I got all the content needed, and this scene is a has-been. Yes, Sarah has it covered completely.

I glance at the bodybuilder, and he's glowing when he declares, "Oh, here comes the media! Great, it's showtime for us!"

When James rolls his eyes, they have a longing, get-me-out-of-here look.

The three of us overhear the fireman talking into his chest walkie-talkie, speaking rapidly. "Yeah, that's so strange. I was standing right there in front of Isaac, talking about what he was planning for meals today, and like that," he says as he snaps his fingers even though the person on the phone obviously can't see it, "he disappeared, right before my eyes. Man, wish you could have been there. It was wild."

The bodybuilder eavesdrops and asks, "No way, just there and then gone?"

The fireman puts his hand over his mic, in all likelihood to prevent others from listening, but it doesn't work. "I swear on my mother's grave," he says, "that's what happened. *Poof,* not there. Only a pile of clothes where he had stood!"

Nosey Al rudely comments, again adding vulgarities, "Wish I was there to see that one. Hey, you should tell that to the news people over there. Can I come with you, and you can mention me being the one to save the kid on the plane? Maybe the boy and lady want to come, too?"

We shake our heads simultaneously, signaling our lack of interest in joining them.

The fireman ends his call and heads to the news truck with the bodybuilder strutting behind him to claim his fifteen minutes of fame.

I wonder what I should do next. Do you like this kid? I do. We seem to think alike, which makes him intelligent in my book. Plus, he appears to be rather mature for his age and has his act together, considering what he just went through.

I do something uncharacteristic of me, especially in this day and age of not trusting anyone—but why not? What have I got to lose? What would you do at this point? I go for it.

Leaning into James with our shoulders barely touching, I speak in a hushed voice, "Hey, my townhouse is right behind us. Do you want to bug-out, away from this crowd?" The words flow without any restraint or caution. "Come over and get a hold of your parents or someone you know? Maybe clean up, get something to drink, and relax for a few minutes before they arrive?" I wish I would've said that I'm married, so he doesn't get the wrong impression.

Oh, I should never have asked him about his parents. How wrong of me! What if they were on the plane with him? I hope he was alone coming or going on a trip. I assume the plane was landing at Bob Hope Airport in nearby Burbank since it was flying lower than those that cross over the Valley and land at LAX. I must not bring up the topic of his parents again—for his sake and mine. Too heavy, too emotional. How insensitive of me, don't you agree?

"Sure," he answers quietly. "My mom and her husband live in Northridge. I was flying back from seeing my dad in San Diego." He speaks in a quiet voice, "My plane was late, so I was supposed to call when we landed." He looks at his iWatch and lets out a big sigh. "Looks like this thing is busted, so I can't call home. Anyway, can I borrow your phone? Mine's, umm, ruined."

Knowing Northridge is only ten or fifteen minutes away, depending on traffic, I realize I made the right decision in allowing him to come into our home because it shouldn't take up a lot of my time. I pull my phone out of my pocket, unlock its security code, note that a text came in from Jeremy asking if I am okay, and hand it to James. As he presses the numbers, I pick up my camera bag and step away from the curb, consciously trying not to invade his privacy. After what the two of us went through, and with Al and the fireman coming over, I don't want any more attention, especially from any television crew.

James talks in a muffled voice as he makes the call. Only once does he look at me and ask for my home address. He speaks into the phone, "Yes, we have been to this complex; it's where Sean used to live." After only a couple of minutes of conversing, he hands me back the phone as quickly as he can. I sense something is disturbing the boy. Do you agree it could have something to do with seeing those dead bodies?

As you can tell, my brain starts working and planning. I'll get James over to our house, give the kid something to drink, let him clean up, and wait with him for his parents or whomever to come get him. It won't take long. It's the least I can do after what he's experienced. I'm glad his parents weren't on the plane. I'm happy he isn't hurt, aren't you?

When he's gone, I'll download the pics for Carl and write up a quick article. By then, Denny will be home, and he'll most likely be upset that I brought a stranger into the house, potentially bringing in who-knows-what virus or disease, but he'll understand. I helped rescue this kid today!

Considering how things went earlier, I feel much better than I did a half-hour ago. It's amazing how in control I can be if I concentrate.

~ Townhouse ~

At least a hundred people are now hanging around the news truck. It's incredible how catastrophes bring people out of their little worlds to hear the sensationalism of others' lives. Turmoil and disaster sell. Carnal gratification sells more, but thank goodness, there are no naked sex scenes here.

After scanning the crowd again for Denny and seeing no sign of him, James and I duck across the playground, avoiding the fireman, Macho Al, and the news crew if they're looking for interviews. I guide the boy as quickly as I possibly can up the walkway.

A shiny hair barrette under the swing catches my eye; I try to ignore it. Did you see it too?

We don't speak much; there are too many people passing us on their way to the crash site, too much noise and confusion. The few words out of my mouth are repeated twice that the unit we live in is "just around the corner." We soon pass our gate and arrive at our front door.

"Wait here, please," I point James to one of the patio chairs. Since I purposely never locked the door for Denny's expected return, I turn the handle and enter our abode, leaving the door ajar. "I'll be right back."

"Denny?" I call out.

How I wish he would answer so we could shift back to our normal lives. I ponder whether I should let James enter or keep him waiting outside. Lately, my husband and I don't let any strangers inside our home. Will it be alright if this boy, who may have a virus or germs, comes into our house? If Denny were here, he'd tell me what to do.

Silence once again responds. Oh, what's the point? Let him get mad. The note I left on top of his cell phone sits untouched. I move it aside and notice the phone has a text message. I set my gear down beside the table, slip off my clogs under it, and retrieve my smartphone out of my pocket, putting it next to Denny's.

"James, sorry." He's still standing in the same spot where I left him. "I wanted to see if my husband was around. He isn't, but I'm sure he'll be back any moment. Come on in."

He doesn't move but says, "Are you sure? I'm up to date on my vaxes." Do you think his words are begging an entrance inside? I find no red flags in their tone, do you? I don't think he is going to viciously attack me or infect me with a virus.

"Yes, I'm sure." I motion him inside. "If you can believe it, I am one of the few who still hasn't tested positive for any of the COVID strains, even though Denny—my husband—did and didn't get super sick. I must have some special gene that keeps it away. But I'm sure if or when I do, it should be a mild case, since I'm fully vaccinated and boosted."

The boy follows me until he stops in the center of the great room. Without speaking, I retrieve two white hand towels from the nearby hall closet next to the bathroom and turn around to offer them to him.

"You sure?" he asks, his brow wrinkled. "These are clean; they'll get dirty from all the ash and soot."

I shake my head, not verbally answering his comment as I reflect on the truth of his statement. A stack of hundreds of bleached white towels can't begin to scrub away the damage done to our memories of the plane crash.

Leading him to the bathroom, I explain, "You can clean up in here. Don't turn on the fan—it's broken and loud." I add, "Oh, wait a sec; I have an idea."

James stands in the bathroom doorway while I head down the hall to the utility room. Several of Denny's clean shirts are folded on the clothes dryer; I pull a dark blue one with a white Zipper Cable logo off the stack and retrace my steps.

"My husband's a consumer electronics sales rep." I hand the shirt over. "He has at least three of these, so this one's all yours. It may be a little big for you, but it'll do for now."

James thanks me as he steps into the room and closes the door.

Knowing it'll take him a few minutes to clean up, I peruse the great room. No obvious changes. The broken Alexa remains in pieces by the fireplace, shaming me for my outburst. Sounds of running water emanate from the bathroom.

Maybe Denny ran out of the townhouse, was at the crash, and tried borrowing a phone to call his. But why wouldn't he try calling me first? Only Mom called my phone.

I grab Denny's phone from the entry hall table.

One text message.

Clicking the access button, I read: *Call me now!* on the screen. I note it came from his golfing buddy, John—the cop.

Denny and I have the same make and model of phone. He has grilled me about every feature on them, so I know exactly how they work. After entering his access password (yes, we do share that private information between us), I click on John's name and hit "Return" and wait for the phone to ring.

He answers on the second ring. "John Malcolm." His voice is deep and gruff.

"John, it's Sarah. I saw you left a message for Denny. Have you heard from him?"

"No." His voice shoots out like a dagger.

"Well, I don't know where he is." I can't believe I'm saying that.

"I called to tell both of you to stay put," John speaks, his voice softening. "The police department is on high alert over all the reports of missing people we're getting recently. If you can manage it, don't leave your house for at least the next couple of days. We got problems out on the streets. I got probs."

"Missing?"

"Yeah. The Missing Person Reports are already starting to pile up."

"Missing persons?" I swallow hard.

"It's crazy," he says. "You wouldn't believe what happened to Carlos and me about a half-hour ago on a Code 10-54d, a possible dead body in Mission Hills."

I'd like him to focus on finding Denny, but he keeps talking: "male, late sixties, probable heart attack, lying on his bedroom floor." He starts talking faster as if he's reading a report to his sergeant. "Carlos gets out his cell and starts accessing our online portal to report it. I recheck the guy for a pulse. Right as I'm touching the deceased's carotid artery with my gloved hand, I hear a strange high-pitched sound. And then—I still can't believe it—the old man disintegrates right before my eyes." Do you visualize him shaking his head in confusion like I'm doing?

John pauses and catches his breath. I wonder if he should be telling me about this police business. Do you think, like me, that he sounds like he's making an urgent confession to a priest? Guess I am the only priest he can find.

"The dead guy is gone, Sarah. Right there, right while I had my hand on his throat, checking for a pulse—gone. His dentures and hearing aids were there, right next to my hand. Found a knee prosthesis and his wallet bulging from his empty pants."

"No way." Is John losing his mind? There's no way this could've happened. Would you believe him? Is he telling us the truth? I question how the cop, a friend of ours, says these things so calmly. I'd be freaking out and rolled up in a ball under my bed covers. Wouldn't you?

"Yep. It did happen. I saw it; I felt it." He continues, "Stay home, Sarah. Hunker down until I call you again. As I said, things are weird out here. I gotta go. Bet there'll be rioting next. Tell Denny what I saw."

John clicks out of the call before I have a chance to question, retort, agree, or mention that I haven't talked to Denny since dinner or that the plane crashed. I put the phone back on the table. What should I do or think next?

This is bizarre. The dead guy disappeared. Like those girls, maybe? And the fireman's coworker?

What's your opinion? What do you think happened? You've been with me all this time. You've seen all that's been going on; do you have any ideas?

James stands in front of the opened bathroom door, wearing Denny's oversized T-shirt that makes his posture look more deflated. Slung over his shoulder is the dirty orange polo. "Where do you want me to put these?" he asks without looking up, each hand gripping a soiled towel.

"Here, I'll take them." I return to the utility room and drop the dirty towels into the trash instead of the washing machine. Unlike my prior struggle with blood-soiled clothing from when the governor's son was shot, this time I discard the items with acceptance and acknowledgment. The towels can be replaced, yet those who died in that airplane crash never will be.

I grab a recycled plastic grocery bag for his shirt from the cupboard.

The door into the garage is next to the dryer. Wondering if Denny went somewhere in his car, I quickly peek inside the darkened room. Nope. His gray BMW SUV and my yellow VW Bug are still parked side by side, safe from the outside world.

I retrace my steps down the hall to find James standing still, both hands deep in his pants pockets. Don't you think he looks out of place?

Glancing up the stairs to the office door, I call Denny's name again. No reply.

I explain to James that I haven't seen my husband since before the plane crash and that we were not on the best of terms. Does it seem odd that I would tell him this? I'm hoping that divulging our marital tiff will break the ice that has refrozen between this boy and me. But it doesn't seem to—he's still silent.

"You look better." I hand him the plastic bag and invite him to use it for his shirt. "Want something to eat or drink? A La Croix or water? Gatorade? Sorry, no Coke or energy drinks are allowed in this house since we think they're too toxic. I do have some leftover lasagna." Is it obvious that I am talking too much, possibly out of my own nervousness?

"A La Croix would be fine, ma'am. Thanks."

"Great. We have orange and berry. Which one?"

After he makes his selection, I suggest, "Why don't you come sit down over here?" And offer him a stool at the kitchen island. He tucks his shirt in the bag and loops it over the metal back of the chair. I move my closed laptop to the far end of the counter by the other stool.

"Your parents should be here shortly. It's been at least five minutes since you called."

"You mean my mom and her husband," he corrects me with a more determined tone. "She divorced Dad two years ago and married him last February. He's okay, I guess. A Black guy who's trying hard to have a White stepson." I sense pain in his voice when he adds, "None of them really wants me."

To avoid looking directly at him, I power up my laptop so I can send the videos over to Carl. While the device starts to synchronize, I grab a tumbler from the cupboard next to the sink.

"Hey," he asks, "do you mind if I use your phone again—check my email, post a comment on Instagram, to tell everyone I am okay?"

"Of course not." I know today's teens are into instant communication, and I feel sorry that James has lost his main connection to his social life and the entire galaxy. "But let's have you do it on my husband's phone."

You'd do the same thing for this kid if you could, right? It's not like he's going to steal any of our personal information.

I retrieve Denny's phone, enter its password, and hand it over to James, and he thanks me again. His lifeline restored, he slides back onto the stool and starts clicking away on the phone. I occupy myself by filling the plastic cup with ice from the refrigerator door, popping open the can, and pouring the drink.

When I deliver the beverage, complete with a coaster, I grab a glance over James's shoulder to see what's absorbing his attention. It's a Twitter account. He looks like the typical teen, safely sheltered in his online world.

"Feel free to check your email, too," I tell him. "I need to make a phone call. I'll be right back."

He thanks me for the drink, using the "ma'am" word again. After taking a couple of gulps, he repeats a "thank you" for the use of the phone.

I go back to the table by the front door and pick up my phone again. I must tell Carl I'll be uploading the pics and videos in minutes. I know I've got great shots and film. The still of James's hand caught mid-wave should get me the praise I deserve.

A voice message and two text messages appear on the phone's screen. Another call from Mom. This time, she left a message, but I'll listen to it later.

Tapping the screen to see who the texts came from, I notice one is from my friend, Zoey. It reads: *Date left me hanging.* I bet she's got a tale to tell about this new guy she met on an online dating site; he must've stood her up. I'll respond when I have time. Jeremy texts, *What's going on?* I ignore that one, too.

I give Carl a call but get the office's primary answering system. Voicemail? Their phone lines must be swamped. As I wait for the automatic message to complete, I think about how the Internet has switched newspapers to online and audio, but someone, somewhere, still likes to read a physical paper. I'm glad Carl had the foresight years ago to merge our news with the interactive website so it could stay in business.

After hitting four numbers to access Carl's voice mailbox, I leave the message: "Carl, Sarah. Uploading 'wow' footage of the plane crash in a few minutes. One survivor. Check out the hand waving. Call or text when you can."

I consider calling Mom back but wait. I'll first get James out of the house and upload the photos. If everything has gone as wacky as John says, I don't need to listen to one of her panic attacks. Like many moms, she can go off the deep end if there's even a minor medical emergency. If a few people are missing, she may be panic-stricken by now.

And you would think by now that Denny, if he had a brain, would contact his wife somehow, some way, and tell me he is okay, wouldn't you? Ugh. That man!

Plus, I'm surprised Aunt Amy hasn't called with another one of her told-you-so doomsday reports.

Ah, yes, maybe this is the end of the world as she'll claim it to be.

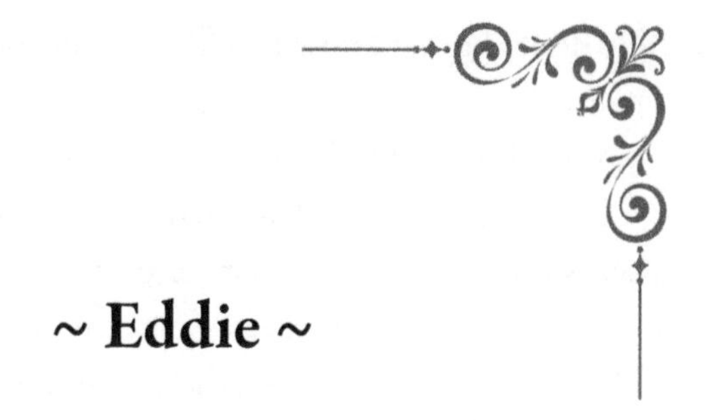

~ Eddie ~

When I return to the kitchen, I find James sitting with both hands gripping his drink. Denny's phone has a blackened screen and rests unused.

"Done already?" I ask, wanting to break into his thoughts.

James releases the cup and puts both hands on his pant legs, repeatedly rubbing the fabric. He bows his head.

"Anything wrong? Anything I can do?" I don't want to hear his answer yet and consider mentioning my job since he had shown interest in it and my camera. But at the same time, I want to learn everything about the plane crash. Don't you?

Before I can speak, he whispers wistfully, "Eddie."

"I see. Is he your friend, brother, dad?" I want to know but feel I'm as intrusive as the television crew outside. Do you think it could be about his parents divorcing?

"The guy next to me."

"Oh." That could change the dynamics. Did he know this person or not? Does this relate to the plane crash?

Do you think I should ask more? Am I being too nosy?

Trying not to pry, I stutter to get the words out, "O-on the plane?"

James rubs his eyes as I sit down on the stool next to him. I want to put my hand on his shoulder, to comfort him, but I can't do it; I don't know this kid. I want to ask but don't know what to say. I want to know who this person is or was to James. I wait for him to speak again.

Daddy taught me that—whoever is silent the longest in a discussion usually gets what he or she wants from the other person by letting him speak first, even if there's a long lapse. Unfortunately, I rarely use the technique; it's quite hard for me to keep my mouth shut for any period (unless, of course, it involves an argument with my husband, then I can be as tight-lipped as Denny is. I'm on to him). But at this second, it's the only idea that comes to mind. Have you ever tried it?

I wait, arduously attempting not to be a journalist for once in my life. Wanting to be a friend or confidant—something I'm not comfortable doing, ever. I feel out of my element, allowing this kid to think that he controls the conversation.

Finally, after what seems like three days of dead air, James looks at me. His eyes are bloodshot. Has he been crying?

"He was in the seat next to me, next to the window. A guy who I'd just met."

I presume this Eddie was in the crash; maybe the poor kid saw him die. That would be enough to cave me. His distress makes sense. I bet even you'd be more up a creek without a paddle than this boy, wouldn't you?

I keep silent, consciously clenching my molars.

"We're talking about the Lakers and other basketball teams, you know, guy stuff. Who he liked and didn't like, teams we hope go to the finals. He was cool; he offered to give me tickets to next Friday's game since he can't use his season passes." He twiddles his thumbs in his lap.

"Is he your age?" I ask, contributing minimally.

"Older, lots older, guessing twenties. Dunno."

"Hmm. Go on."

James starts to bounce his left knee up and down nervously. I can feel it slightly vibrate through the floor.

"Since we were getting ready to land, he gave me a pen to write down my email address on one of those napkins the flight attendants give you. Saying he would send me the tickets later. I was right next to him. And, and ..."

Here I imagine it's at this point that the plane started to fall from the sky; it's tilted, and everyone was holding on for dear life, or perhaps there was an onboard fire.

"I handed the napkin to him. He took it and was starting to put it and a candy bar into the pocket of the back of the seat in front of him, where he kept his wallet."

"Uh-huh." It's like pulling teeth to get this kid to spit out what he wants to say. What did Daddy tell me? Oh, yeah, say only "really, uh-huh, and oh" if you want someone to keep talking. Don't voice your opinion. I'd never believed in such a theory, but I try it.

"Oh?" I add.

"Have you ever watched any of the *Star Trek* movies?" That was unexpected. I wonder if the kid hit his head on something and lost his marbles when the plane crashed. "You know, the movies with Captain Kirk and Spock?"

"Uh-huh." There is a pause, but I must add my two cents worth, "Of course, my husband is a Trekkie fan." There's a hint of pride in my tone while I ignore my thoughts of the boy being delusional by going totally off-topic. I don't care for the iconic genre or its silliness and lack of logic, but I know of the television series and all the movies, along with their characters and plots, since Denny drags me to the theater every time a new flick releases.

"You know about the transporter and how it can instantly take one person from one place to another?"

"Yup, like 'Beam me up, Scottie' and Kirk hits that communicator on his chest to go back to the spacecraft—a strange concept, but it'd be neat to have one instead of taking a car or plane to get somewhere. Denny could use it for his sales calls." Do you have any idea why we're talking about this? "Think how much time he'd save not being in Valley traffic."

I'm not following my father's advice of being quiet, am I? I'm taking over the conversation again. I know you're thinking, shut up, Sar, and let him talk.

"Okay, picture that." He pauses to take a big gulp of his drink.

I squint my eyes, trying to connect the dots, but I don't get it. How does a transformer correlate to an airplane crash? Would you happen to know?

"Let me backtrack." He rubs his forehead as though massaging the vision will clear in his memory.

Goodness, get on with the story, kid! What happens next? This is insane. Are you getting as flustered as I am?

Is he worried I will make fun of him or mock him?

"Eddie had a cast on his left arm because he cracked a bone snowboarding and was looking forward to getting it off next week. He was putting a candy bar and the napkin I wrote on in the seat pocket, but somehow the edge of his cast got stuck in the webbing, so he makes some comment about how nothing is easy. I look over at the guy, and he's laughing. And then, like in a second, he vanishes right while I'm staring at him." He mutters the words. They're full of fear and uncertainty.

"Really?" is all I can reply, thinking of what John had told me about the dead man who disappeared when he was touching him.

"But it wasn't like the transporter in *Star Trek*." James's right knee is banging up and down now. "There was no swirling of brightly colored molecules into a circle that disappears into nothing—no, nothing like that. He left his clothes. There, right there, on his seat. Even the cast on his arm bounced off the seat backing and may have rolled behind us!"

"No!" I cover my mouth with my hand in unbelief.

"And his sunglasses on top of his head, well, they fell on top of his clothes. I mean, I was looking at the candy bar, which I watched fall to the floor, but I could see him too. His face, hands, and body, all of it disappeared—just gone. *Poof.* Nothing was left of him, of his body. It didn't disintegrate or fade away. He went away in an instant. I was so freaked out; I even dropped the pen that I was holding."

The analytical side of me takes the realistic approach. "James, don't take this the wrong way, but maybe you suffered head trauma. Did you hit your head on anything right before he supposedly disappeared? Or are you on any medications or drugs that could have made you think you saw this?" I tap my fingers nervously on the counter, hoping he's not a psycho who forgot to take his pills on time and is ready to attack me in my house and leave me for dead. "Or you thought you saw this; maybe you were under too much stress."

The teen unlocks his hands and slams a fist on the granite, causing little tremors in his drinking container. "No!" He leaps to his feet. "This happened before the crash, right when there was a strange sound throughout the plane. And I don't do drugs, and I'm not on anything. You weren't there, but I saw it. I saw Eddie disappear!"

Scared he'll react more violently with further questioning, I immediately respond, "Okay, no problem, just a thought." I change the subject, "Want another La Croix?" I stand up, too, ready to flee if the situation goes south.

He runs his hands through his hair. "You don't believe me, do you? No one will. I must be crazy. Mom will send me back to her weird analyst, therapist, or whatever they call them. I know it. This'll make me even more screwed up." He plops back down on the chair and rubs both red eyes again. "Fine, don't believe me, but I know what I saw."

I'm thinking the same thing you are. This kid needs help. He's in shock.

"I should've asked Eddie more questions."

What's he talking about now?

As I sit back down, the kid looks at me, calm and collected. Just like that he switched to a different personality. How can he flip-flop from being so out of whack to being under total control? I thought I had the conversation-domination issue down to a science, but this boy is good, especially for his age. All the more reason to like him.

He slowly turns his cup in a half-circle on its coaster. "Eddie was telling me things earlier on the flight, and I have no clue what they mean. He asked me if I believed in God, and I told him there's never been any discussion about any kind of religion in our house, even after my parents divorced. As a matter of fact, I've never been to a talk or sermon or whatever you call them unless you consider weddings or funerals. There's nothing of that, never has been. All my parents ever did was fight and yell. Eddie was saying how I can know God and have peace and that kinda stuff. I'm a lost soul, he said. I don't know what he was talking about, but he sounded so sure of himself, so, um, happy—or what's that word? Contented. Yeah, he said he was content. He told me I should read the Bible, said everything's in there."

Irritated by the mention of the topic, I interrupt, "Stop, please, James. Stop. I've heard all about religion, and don't you believe any of it; it's hogwash. You need to forget about what Eddie told you. I know about God and Jesus and the Bible, and it's all a farce. It's all untrue; please don't believe it. Please, let's talk about something else."

I think I've had enough. Have you yet? No religion, remember.

Ladies and gentlemen, what's with this theme today of all days?

I pointedly change the subject again, reverting to my journalist role. "Do you know what happened to the plane? Did you hear a thump or see an engine blow?" I recall not seeing any flames when the plane whizzed by the townhouse's windows.

"No, no thud or bump. Flying along, and a sudden dip downward, then a turn on its side, and a crash. It happened so fast." He reports the words mechanically, apparently still super-glued to Eddie's religious conversation. "Never heard so many people scream. It was awful." He closes his eyes for a long time, perhaps reliving the memory. Or maybe trying to purge it.

"Did the pilot or crew tell you what had happened?"

"No, no time to. First, a weird noise and Eddie disappearing, and next some lady comes on the overhead speaker screaming something real fast like, 'We need a pilot! Emergency! Brace yourselves!' By then, the plane had rolled on its side. Everything was falling all around us inside the plane. I got hit in the back of my head by something soft, like a purse or carry-on bag. It wasn't someone's laptop or tablet. I remember after it that my shoulder hit the seat in front of me, and I slumped downward."

"Are you bleeding? Where were you hit in the head? Want me to check?" The thought of looking for blood in his hair makes me queasy, but I offer to do so out of worry.

"No, I checked in the mirror in the bathroom and couldn't find any blood; only a bump right here." He points to the back of his head, shrugs, and then takes a drink of his La Croix.

Silence falls between us.

While staring at his tumbler, I formulate more questions in my head. I speculate what the pilot was doing, where he was, and why he didn't have control of the plane. Did something happen to him? Why else would the flight attendant ask if there was a pilot on board? Could this be terrorism? After 9/11, you never know. Why was there neither fire nor smoke? Do you think this boy may have a concussion since he admits to being clunked in the head? There are so many unresolved answers.

Mesmerized by his story, I'm dying to know how the event happened, especially since I also heard an unusual sound. Maybe it came from the plane, but John had mentioned it, too.

How weird that we all heard it—including you—and at the same time!

I organize my thoughts to figure out which angle to take in writing the article on the plane crash. Should it be from the perspective of the only person to survive the crash, this polite, poised fifteen-year-old or the confused, hit-in-the-head teenager who says he saw a guy disappear before his eyes right before the plane did its deathly nosedive? Was there a pilot flying the plane? Are you as confused as I am?

James brings me back to the present, continuing with stubborn determination. "But I'll never, ever, ever forget what happened to Eddie, and I promise, I'm gonna read that Bible from start to finish and find out what he was talking about. He knew something; I know he did."

Thankfully, our doorbell rings, rescuing me from having to yank him out of his Biblical trance.

~ Parent ~

"James! Get out here right this minute!" Although the voice is female, it's powerfully piercing the closed door.

I open it quickly. You can see her, right? A perfectly dressed, perfectly postured woman wearing a sparkly designer N95 face mask. She's older than I am; I'm guessing she's in her mid-to-late forties. Her dyed blonde hair is styled to the point it wouldn't dare move thanks to all the hairspray. A couple of wrinkles are visible on the skin that shows around her mask. Her neatly creased, white capri pants, probably Ann Taylor or J. Crew, match well with her navy-blue-and-white-striped crepe sleeveless shirt. She's wearing an oversized blue marble-designed necklace with matching earrings and a bracelet.

Now, don't you start thinking I'm jealous of her; I'm only giving you my graphic description of her opulent attire—an outfit I could never pull off correctly. She's the essence of fashion. A size two or smaller—what I'm clearly not. No judging me by my perception of her, as it's merely facts. Look for yourself and see what I mean.

"James!" she demands again in a loud squeal. "What are you thinking being in a stranger's house? Haven't I told you before that you have no clue if people we don't know can contaminate us? Get out here this minute."

As fast as possible, I grab the bohemian mask that I had tucked in my pocket when cleaning the drawer and fasten its loops on my ears. Without speaking, I point to the box of unused medical masks on the nearby table; James rushes to retrieve one and puts it on. Avoiding entering the townhouse, the woman backs up five feet and stands on the patio near the table and chairs, expecting us to join her.

With the government's mask mandates no longer in effect, it's a free-choice issue. I understand where this woman is coming from and why. She doesn't know me; she's protecting her son and herself from possible viruses and germs. No, I don't fault her thinking. Denny and I still wear masks when we know someone has the flu, a stomach bug, or a cold, or when we're put in a precarious situation around those who are coughing or sneezing constantly, especially if it's a closed-in area like a crowded stadium or sports arena. I get it. COVID was horrible and killed too many; it's still a problem worldwide, with one after another variant continually taunting us. Aunt Amy, of course unvaxed, almost died of it when she was in the hospital on a ventilator. She pulled through. If it's not one virus, it'll be another. Look what's happening with polio, smallpox, and monkeypox. Be smart and be safe. Please, we don't want to go through another pandemic.

As if needing time to restore her decorum, the woman clears her throat, then looks down at her large platinum wedding ring with an oversized diamond that shows off her French-tipped nails. She looks back up, asking, "Sarah Colton?"

"Yes," I reply, trying to inflect compassion in my voice. "I'm glad you came so fast." I join her on the patio, James following me. "Gee, your son sure had a scare today."

She rushes around me to her son and awkwardly hugs him. He appears embarrassed; his eyes do not meet hers, but he puts a hand loosely around her diminutive frame.

"Jimmy, I'm so happy you didn't get hurt! What a nightmare you must've been through, my poor baby." The fake-and-bake woman stiffly tries to comfort him, probably not wanting to mess up her clothes or hair.

He isn't allowed time to respond.

"I would've been here earlier except for the traffic. I was driving down Zelzah Avenue by Cal State Northridge, and it's down to one lane each way. At least twenty or thirty college students were standing in the street. At first, I thought there was a protest or march or even a riot again, but there was a car stalled out, and it must've backed up traffic to Devonshire Street. The guys were rocking a green Suburban back and forth to move it out of the way. Broke down right there on the spot, I guess."

She switches her silver-studded purse that could hold my camera bag and all the contents of our dreaded junk drawer to her other shoulder and steps back from James. She inspects him, trying to spot any bruises or marks on his body without making contact. "Don't know where the driver was or why no one thought to get in the car. When I finally drove by it, I heard one boy say the car was locked, abandoned right in the middle of the road. People these days, thinking only of themselves."

James and I can't get an "oh" in edgewise as she prattles on. "Then, right before I got to the elementary school, there was a school bus flipped on its side by that strip mall near Rinaldi Street. It looked like there were no children around; hope it was empty before it crashed."

She's still not finished.

"My car radio said there're big traffic problems everywhere. Even had one of those broadcast emergency warnings on my cellphone seconds ago as I stood waiting by your gate. Planes crashing, boats sinking, people gone—I wonder what happened. We'll have to turn on the news when we get you home, dear."

Even though she's mentioning interesting stuff, are you getting tired of her monologue, too? I keep myself occupied by inspecting her perfect pedicure peeping out from her silver-and-blue-stone sandals.

She takes a closer look at her son. "James, where'd you get this T-shirt?" She pinches the clothing. "Did your father give it to you? Couldn't he pick out a smaller size, one that fits you?"

"No, Mom. It's Sarah's—I mean Ms. Colton's—husband's. She said I could have it. I still have the orange polo, the one you gave me. Probably ruined, it's pretty dirty." He looks at me, eyebrows raised, like asking for permission to venture back inside to retrieve it.

"I'll get it." Welcoming any excuse to escape their conversation, I go into the house, grab the bagged shirt from the stool, retrace my steps, and hand it off to the woman. She pulls the garment out for inspection.

"Well, that's too bad. I'll see if Juanita can remove the stains." She casts her gaze on me and speaks woman-to-woman. "Our housekeeper knows so many cleaning tricks. And you know how hard it's to get good help these days."

She considers her son again. "And where exactly is your backpack, Jimmy?"

"Mom, it's gone. I-I lost it during the crash. And my iWatch is busted." He holds up his wrist to confirm the timepiece's destruction.

"Oh, right," the woman says with an exasperated sigh. "We'll have to file an insurance claim for your clothes, watch, and electronics. I'm sure that'll get us nowhere, but we should try as soon as possible. These things are all rather pricey, after all, especially those Nordstrom pants and Ray-Ban sunglasses. Why aren't you wearing them? The glasses were from your stepfather."

James ignores her, bringing her back to the present. "Mom, Ms. Colton works for the newspaper. Since she took pictures of the crash, they may be in the news."

"That's nice. I'm so glad you didn't get injured," she repeats. She tries to push a wayward hair out of her son's face, but he winces and retreats a few feet, brushing against one of the patio chairs. He runs his fingers through his hair nervously; he cringes a bit when they touch the goose egg on the back of his head.

She recovers from the slight by continuing her soliloquy. "I called your father but had to leave a voice message again. You know he's never around, probably out selling his blasted roofs after he dropped you off at the airport. He just can't make enough money, can he? Anyway, I told him that you're unharmed."

James puts his hands in his pockets and doesn't react to the criticism of his dad. With an unresponsive audience, she seems to run out of things to say, don't you think?

Finally, James turns to me, "Ma'am—I mean Sarah—thanks again for the drink and someplace to clean up. It was nice of you."

The mother turns the conversation back to herself. "Art would've come, James." She lays her hand on his forearm. "You know how hard he's trying to get used to having a son. He really wanted to come. He sends his love."

James disregards her words but allows his mother's touch.

"He was getting the Tesla out of the garage so we could drive over together, but the hospital paged him."

She looks to me again, for confirmation or to impress me—I don't know which. "You know how OB/GYN doctors' schedules are," she tells me. "He oversees the department so must be on call 24/7. I'm so proud of what he does."

Our eyes meet. Did you spot a tinge of insecurity as she quickly glanced away? Now it makes sense to me—James's mother is a trophy wife and recently "upgraded" her husband, as Zoey would describe it. I surmise that a doctor is much better suited for her lifestyle than a roofing salesperson. Right?

"He called back while I was on my way here. There were several emergencies all at the same time. Dr. Abraham is upset, something about a baby disappearing from his hands in the delivery room. And how the entire newborn floor is empty, no babies." Her words register, but she says them without restraint as if she's at the salon getting pampered, bragging about her latest adventures. At least that's how I interpret the tone of her voice.

I know you want me to ask more, but James beats me to the punch, "Yeah, been there, done that, Mom. There's something to all these missing people, and I'm going to find out what it is."

"Jimmy, you're a kid." She shakes her head at his confidence. "What can you do?"

He repeats his words slowly and emphatically. "I'm going to find out."

"Fine, son. But first, let's get home. I left a bunch of groceries on the counter and need to put them away as I couldn't find Juanita."

After grabbing the pen and the same envelope I used for Denny's note from the hall table, I have James write down his phone number on the back of the paper in case I need to contact him. He thanks me once again, but his mind seems to be on other things—otherworldly things, perhaps.

We bid our goodbyes, and when they leave, I'm relieved the woman is gone. I hope James will be able to deal with the crash, Eddie, and his family situation in a healthy manner. A grief counselor might do him some good rather than that "reading the Bible" nonsense, wouldn't you think?

Finally, you and I are alone with my thoughts and can concentrate on the questions of the day: Why hasn't Denny returned, and what's all this about people missing? And babies? No newborns? Surely that hasn't happened. It couldn't be true if there are no children alive on the planet.

I flinch, aware that I may have been pregnant less than an hour ago. Is that what could've happened to me?

Determined to stave off any panic wanting to detonate inside me, I center on being circumspect and having common sense.

What do you think?

~ Internet ~

You can tell my mind is fired up. While I'm uploading the videos, I'll call Carl again. I must talk to him. He'll give me the dirt on everything, including the missing people.

Shutting the front door, I don't lock the deadbolt in case Denny returns. Accessing my gear bag again, I take out my coveted video card. I grab the other card out of my camera and make a beeline for my laptop on the island counter.

"Denny?" I call, half-heartedly to the still air as I pass the staircase. Wonder where he factors in today's events. Did he leave when I was in the bathroom? Is this a joke to him? Did he see the airplane crash from the upstairs office window? Or is he in one of his pouts? Where did he go?

What would you do if you couldn't figure out where your spouse was during a crisis, especially after you got into an argument and are no longer speaking? You probably think it's weird that I'm not upstairs pounding on the door or entering his sacred space uninvited. Maybe it is weird, but I'm the type that stands my ground—I don't cave, period. I'm rarely the first person to break the silence in a disagreement and reconcile. If he can hear all this chaos and can't be bothered to take a moment to make sure I'm alright, then let him stew in his own juices. That's my attitude, anyway. You may have a different opinion, but I'm the one in charge here. You're only an observer in my brain; I'm not in yours.

And, by the way, we are not strangers to conjugal disputes. We're like all normal couples. We have arguments, just like you do with someone you love. There is something seriously wrong with a relationship if there are no fights from time to time.

Take two years ago: We got into a clash over household chores since we both work and have little time for such nonsense. We each stated our cases, and I debated in a confrontational yet unattached, manner. Denny left without a murmur and without packing a bag—only to call my cell the next day acting as if nothing had happened. Never found out where he spent the night. Maybe Aunt Amy's house. Then, last year, the day after Christmas, we fought over having children. He wants them, and I don't, at least not yet. Especially since the scare earlier today. He stormed out mid-sentence, gone who knows where for six hours. It fries me how he acts when he thinks he's right and I'm wrong. But he came back; Denny always comes back. Where is he now, and am I supposed to think everything is my fault? I love the man dearly, but he can be frustrating sometimes. Sorry, I'm not conceding yet, especially since I know I am right.

Maybe he's got a girlfriend on the side nearby and went to be with her since I'm such a sinful person. Could be that saucy Brittany from work finally got her claws into him, and they met somewhere. Never know; my advice is don't trust anyone.

Or it could be that he walked out to the plane crash and is at the television van, yakking away with Mr. Muscleman and the fireman or helping someone in need. If so, we must have missed seeing each other somehow in the crowd. I must believe that—nothing bad has happened to him, and surely, he can't be one of the so-called missing.

I tell myself not to worry. I'll hang tight and keep waiting for him to come back.

Knowing it's faster to upload on a laptop than on a smartphone, I hit the "Ctrl" and "H" buttons on the hibernating keyboard. My laptop comes to life, displaying my server page's website, the *Valley News* portal to the world.

The Internet is an amazing tool. Who would have dreamed up such instant information a hundred years ago? It's beyond comprehension that, since the early 1900s, we barely had automobiles, televisions, and airplanes. Now, a little over a hundred years later, we're speaking into smartphones that auto-text while we drive our fully-loaded mini-rooms, communicate at warp speed via the Internet instead of snail-mail or a corded telephone, and fly around the cosmos to the space station. Makes me think of something Aunt Amy likes to say. I can't remember the exact wording, but it is something like this: "Many shall run to and fro, and knowledge shall be increased." Well, technology certainly has expanded our knowledge. No doubt about it, people are running around trying to dissect and inspect every iota of our lives. Truly a wonderful time to be alive in the history of the world.

Although they can be challenging at times, I love the advances of modern technology, don't you? I mean, here you are in my head right now—it's strange, but how awesome is that?

I stare at the screen: An emergency broadcast alert of white letters on a black background catches my attention, especially when bold headlines scroll across the top of the page, stopping my concentration.

Many Missing.

Where Are the Children?

Planes, Trains, and Automobile Madness.

UFOs or a Virus?

Photographs are systematically changing on the screen in front of me. Flashing mere seconds, one at a time.

Flash.

Homes burning.

Flash.

Two planes in mid-air collision above an airport landing strip.

Flash.

Multiple cars piled up on a freeway.

Flash.

Train derailed in Germany.

Flash.

Empty daycare center.

Flash.

Cruise liner in the Caribbean crashing into a dock.

Flash.

A chemical formula with the words "Another Pandemic?" next to it.

Flash.

UFOs spotted.

Flash.

Police in uniforms wearing terrorism gear, gas masks, and shields.

Flash.

Do you see these pictures? Do you know what's happening? Can you tell me what's going on here, everywhere?

One picture after another, changing to the next shocking scene. Like flipping through a book on catastrophes, one after another after another. Full color. Some cover the screen with no words or comments provided.

A video pops up on the screen. It's a broadcast-news scene, but I can't tell if it's national or local. A smartly dressed Asian newscaster sits behind a glossy black desk with backdrops of major cities behind him. Although the video is muted, the man is obviously discussing the progress of pollution and global warming over the last fifty years based on the displayed pictures on the screen. The soundless video slows down, showing frame by frame. The speaker looks directly at me—well, technically, the television camera. His lips stop moving, and he glances slightly upward. Then he's no longer there. It's instantaneous—in one twenty-fifth of a second. Gone. The newscaster's shirt, tie, and suit jacket slink down on the desk, slowly dropping out of view. His wristwatch teeters back and forth on the shiny counter, fully latched. His earpiece drops to the empty chair where he once sat. The body is gone.

It's precisely as James and John described.

The video ends. It's incredible. My mind refuses to accept what I've viewed. There must be an explanation. But what? Was it a magic trick?

Your input, please?

Next, a chart pops up of a map of the world. It shows color-coded regions indicating where people have reportedly vanished so far. Seems like the United States, England, and parts of Australia have the largest counts so far.

The Internet is a plethora of instant information, but this is utterly bizarre.

I click over to an all-the-time national news site. More pictures and video clips, some the same as what I've just seen, others showing entirely new problems. Increasingly strange happenings and weird occurrences. All had occurred at the same moment in time.

I stare at the flashing words and images, astounded by how quickly—guessing it's been over an hour—so much information has been uploaded.

In my lifetime, in yours, nothing like this has happened before, causing so many problems at once in every corner of the globe.

It's a journalist's field day.

We're a part of it. Yes, you are, too. Are you as awed as I am?

I'm here, watching it.

You and I must never forget this moment.

This is history. We are history.

And yes, my dear, Sarah-girl is in control.

~ Carl ~

Ignoring the emergency alert post on my cellphone, I hit the speaker button and call Carl again, hoping not to get a machine.

"Valley News." Good. I recognize the receptionist's voice. Brittany the flirt.

"It's Colton. Patch me to Carl." As usual, my words are brusque when speaking to her. But this time, the horrific scenes displayed on my laptop divert my attention.

"In a sec," she replies in the same short, brash pitch as mine.

The photos keep flipping in front of me.

A wailing mother holds a light blue baby blanket.

A picture of a movie star's daughter with the caption "Disappeared" printed on a flyer.

Several groups starting to gather outside of the U.S. Capitol and the White House, maybe already seeking answers or demanding action.

I think of the show, *The Twilight Zone.* This evening's events would make a great movie if you could capture the freakiness of it. Are you as blown away as I am by how fast the news has been posted for the world to see? All thanks to high-speed, instant communication.

I finally hear Carl's voice. "Sar—I'm busy," he complains curtly.

"Sorry, uploading video in a few," I say. "When's the deadline, so I can do a write-up?"

"Don't bother. Got too much feed; there's no room for words. Text me only details, no fluff. Send over videos ASAP. George will upload them to our website, and we'll dovetail them with brief descriptions. Been using Meta so far and want a local approach on our page. You got survivors?"

"Only one—exclusive, too." I'm glad James avoided the television crew.

"Great, send away. Is Jeremy with you?"

"Jeremy? No, why?" Yes, we stick close together at work; he's a video technician so is always giving me tips. We're the same age, born in the Valley, and have many things in common, except I'm married, and he's not.

"Just wondering. He left about fifteen minutes ago. I thought he was headed your way to the crash. No doubt rattled about what's happening. But he also told Brittany he needed to go to Encino to check on his parents."

"I did get a text from him while I was at the crash, but I didn't see him in the field. Doubt he's there, but other news vans arrived. Checking on his parents makes sense. I'll text him when we hang up."

"Thanks," answers Carl, obviously distracted. I can hear several people in the background vying for his attention.

"I may have a follow-up story," I add, trying to bait his curiosity. "The kid and I bonded." I suggest it because I'd love to do a feature article on James and mention that Eddie guy.

"We'll see." Having worked for my boss for three years, I've never heard him sound defeated. It's not like him.

"Carl, everything all right? You sound off."

He pauses before replying, perhaps weighing his next words. Next, I hear over the phone an office door close; it could be his, because the background noises become muffled.

"I don't want to alarm you, but people have up and disappeared, and no one can say where, why, or how. It's unbelievable, and no one knows anything." Sniffles come from the phone; he could be crying. "Something has happened, something awful.

"Helen is a wreck—she almost got killed on the freeway when a car sped past her at eighty miles an hour with no one at the wheel." I think of his lovely wife and the horror of witnessing such an event. "The car had to be on cruise control with no driver. At least our neighbor got her to take some sedatives a few minutes ago. Then, Frank, you know, the older guy who's temping in records? We found his clothes and stuff at his desk—no Frank." I hear the unmistakable sound of Carl blowing his nose.

"Whoa, that's weird. What's your thought about it?" I put the video card in the port to load the transfer.

"Beats me. At first, missing reports suggested people suddenly being gone from their families or jobs. There were strange crashes and accidents. Then we have these cases of people vanishing in real-time; we even have some incidents on video. So far, there are hundreds of missing people, they estimate, on a national level. But we know it's global and rapidly escalating. I'm unsure what numbers we're talking about, but it all seems to have happened at the same second in time."

"What's the cause?" I ask, baffled; you most likely are, too.

"Who knows? There's a group of scientists suggesting it may have something to do with another strange virus, you know, like an abnormal mutant of COVID or AIDS or the Marburg virus, but far faster and more destructive to the body, making it disintegrate instantly. Maybe a chemical reaction of some sort."

I think of James's description of Eddie in *Star Trek's* transporter.

"Can't figure," Carl continues. "The press is speculating. We've got some real doozies. You know, things the psychics had visions of eons ago only now coming to pass. Then there's a theory about chemicals that entered a hole in the ozone and invaded the planet or another about a solar flare or polar shift erupting its magnetic energy to infect specific individuals. And the Martian-took-over-our-bodies or UFO/aliens-arrived concepts. And, of course, there's the religious idea about the end of the world. Believe me, the list of explanations is expanding. But there must be a scientific answer. Over an hour ago, certain people—in the thousands, perhaps millions—don't suddenly disappear everywhere on the planet. Where did they go, and will they come back?"

I purse my lips tightly and shake my head at this collection of possible explanations as I open my video links and start scanning through them to make sure they're viewable. I should call Aunt Amy and see what she thinks, but I know she'll lash out with her "my God is great" attitude and try to convince me the end of the world's doom and gloom has finally arrived.

She'd gloat with righteous indignation, even if it weren't the exact cause.

After passing the video clip where I noticed the wedged candy bar, it shows James's fingers waving in the zoom-in. Perfect. I'm so thankful I took a still shot at the same time. No need for words when a photo or video shows it all.

Carl mentions the odd sound, recalling he heard it, too, and thought it might have something to do with so many people disappearing.

"Other ideas the scientists are looking at is the common denominator," he says. "A White House communique came in before you called. It's unreal, Sarah. They're inquiring about children under a certain age missing. Up to the age of ten or twelve was a guesstimate. Do you know what that means? There could be no babies in the United States, perhaps the entire world! No kids in elementary school or preschool, no babies being born, no pregnancies. Gone, *kaput*. Every one of them? If so, that's unbelievable. The report specifically asked the press to downplay this angle. We thought COVID was bad, but the impact of this will be something our country or world has never experienced."

I freeze. Did you, too? What about me? Was there a baby inside me or not? I wince at the thought I could have been pregnant today and had been considering an abortion. Me. No cramps now, but I have a sick feeling that I had been carrying a child—Denny's and my child—and I am no longer. Did my baby, our baby, disappear when that sound happened? Could it be possible?

And then there are Jack and Jasmine, my nephew and niece. Did they go, too?

Do you know anyone with young kids? Can you check to see if they're missing?

"I had no idea this was so colossal," I say, trying to block out all images of children and think analytically.

"It is," Carl replies. "Another report mentioned that the vanishing rates seem to be higher among the elderly and the developmentally disabled than those in the twenty to sixty-year-old age group. Explain that. Maybe they have some unique gene configuration."

He pauses and lets out a loud breath. "We're intelligent beings, and we'll figure it out."

I open our online news portal and begin up-linking the videos and stills one at a time. "Scientists can only suggest a new virus?" I ask. "But what do they think causes it, and will it keep happening?"

"These scientists think the virus is the most realistic choice. It may have affected the weaker people of the youngest and eldest generations, but so far, no one knows of any more disappearing acts. Let's hope it's a one-time event, and we don't hear that odd noise again. What I don't understand is why did it happen in the same second and not sporadically over time around the world. To avoid global panic, the White House has asked us to hold back some information; we don't want the public to go berserk, especially about the children. We'll let it leak out slowly, giving people a chance to absorb it bit by bit."

"What else is coming across the Source?" I ask, referring to our massive database. Thanks to incorporating and swapping data with Meta's supercomputer, information is retrieved instantly and efficiently without human interference. It gives us police information, driver's license numbers, registrations, addresses, personal credit card balances, mortgages—anything you want on anyone, there at your fingertips. We read it often and use the information to our benefit. Big Brother is a huge asset to our industry.

"More than you could imagine," Carl says. "It's been dumping data continuously. We can't keep up with the uploading to our website."

All my videos and photos are now online and pasted into the link.

I invite him to check my Source folder. "Got four videos and many pics posted in sequenced time and order. The third one is the best; you can use the still of the kid's hand waving too."

"Thanks. I'll add it to the rest. We've got a ton of cameras on streetlights and buildings and enough car accident videos. But I want to get your plane material so locals can see what's happening in the Valley."

"Great, I'll type up a quick email and send it over with the details."

"Just give bullets. With all this data, we can't run much more."

"Gotcha. Give me a few minutes."

We say our goodbyes. I text Jeremy, asking where he is, and put the cell down on the counter. After closing the news portal, I open my email account.

~ Mom ~

Still seated in the kitchen, I think about my brief to Carl on the plane crash. Keep it simple, Sarah. Simple and concise.

My inbox pops open, and I view my emails within seconds: work, work, junk, coupons, junk.

Ah, this is interesting—an email titled "Sorry." From Aunt Amy, no less.

Hmm. That's funny. I ask you, is it a sorry that she's butting into and ruining my life or a sorry that I need to apologize to her for some sinful act I've committed? Or a sorry about the mess happening worldwide right now? I'll deal with Denny's aunt in a while. I must get the email to Carl pronto.

After opening a new screen, I enter my employee ID number and a blank page appears.

I type "Granada Hills Plane Crash" into the subject line.

Then I write the date, approximate time, and location and mention that the accident happened next to the megachurch so most readers will know its whereabouts. I'm guessing one to two thousand people march hypnotically through its church doors every Sunday; their cars block traffic like you wouldn't believe on the main outlet street. I'm glad the townhouse complex isn't involved in its parking problems. Now that I think about it, the same field where the plane crashed is used for the church's overflow parking. While it had burned during a fire years ago, it has now become a charred graveyard with strewn-out body parts.

My fingers type in James's name and age. The Source is already uploading pictures (including links of those posted on social media), data, and even blood type into separate columns on my screen. In a new section, I add the name of the airport, airline, and estimated landing time, knowing the Source will supply the type of plane, flight number, and how many passengers and crew were aboard. The finely tuned database icon shows its search progression for James's name along with any people involved, famous or not, for any pertinent data. I type in Eddie's name, realizing I don't have a last name. Without asking, the Source spits back any Eddie, Edward, or Ed options to choose from the passenger manifest. An Edward Halstead pops up on the screen, complete with his seat number, age, address, phone, relatives, employment, traffic tickets, et cetera.

Al/Albert King's name is entered in the search list; hopefully, the Source will dig up some dirt on the guy who thinks he's God's gift to the universe because he rescued James. A quick scan shows he's forty-eight years old, married and divorced three times, has a twenty-two-year-old son, owns a gym in Reseda, and rents his townhouse. He owes over eight grand in past-due alimony and back taxes. Oh, and he was arrested several years ago for drunk driving. Stellar guy. Not.

My phone rings once again. Picking it up, I hope with all my heart that it's Denny, somewhere close by, with a reasonable explanation.

Mom.

Ugh. Not now. What's with her?

I swipe the phone and growl without giving her any margin to speak. "Mom, give me a second; I have to finish something important."

"Sarah!" She is not cheery. I hear her screaming something in the background. She's majorly upset. Living in Oregon, my parents seem more demanding of me lately. I think they don't like being far away from either of their daughters, yet they moved there three years ago so Mom could teach graduate geology classes at the University of Oregon.

Leaving my phone on the island, I return to the laptop's keyboard and quickly type in more bullet points about the plane's separated parts, the fire department's arrival, James's hand waving, and Al rescuing the only survivor. I don't bother mentioning my participation or lack of it. After checking for typos and adding the Source's searched data link, I hit the "Send" button.

Finished with the task, I pick up the phone. "Okay, done—whew! Thanks, Mom."

"Sarah!" Her scream hurts my ear. I can tell she's angry that I didn't answer or return her previous calls.

"Sorry, Mom, there was this horrific plane crash in the field next to our condo, and I was one of the first ones on the scene and took videos. This man and I pulled out the only survivor, a teenage boy. I had to finish uploading my images to the paper and ..."

Ignoring me, Mom continues shouting into the phone. "Sarah! You're not listening to me, Sarah! Jack and Jasmine are missing! They're gone!"

She begins sobbing uncontrollably, which turns into coughing. As an asthmatic, Mom knows her allergies have been worse living in the fertile, pollen-filled Willamette Valley, and her symptoms can be problematic.

"No!" I yell back. "Not them! They must be *somewhere*!"

"Silvia is beside herself. The kids were both asleep in their beds, and they are nowhere! They can't find them." Cough. "Just their pajamas, diapers, and blankets. What can we do?" Cough. "Where are they?" The coughing increases. "And poor Silvia—she's home alone—Tom had to leave—trouble at the warehouse." She squeaks the words out between coughs and shallow breaths.

I hear Dad offering her an inhaler, so I tell her not to talk for a few minutes. Meanwhile, I do my best to assure her that the babies will reappear, somehow. I tell her what happened to me and bring her up to date, adding that James's mother came to get him minutes ago.

I hope to soothe her, get her mind on something or someone else, and let her relax the muscles around her agitated airway.

With Silvia being on the opposite coast of the United States, I remind Mom that there's a time difference. She regains somewhat normal breathing without constantly coughing and agrees that there's some logical solution to this puzzle—that the babies will be found, as will the others. I push away the thought of my child no longer being in existence.

"Well, I had a bit of a problem," she stammers in short sentences with only a few sporadic coughs. "I was at Kohl's getting a blouse for our trip. I was standing in line." Cough. "And the cashier disappears! I didn't see her because I was looking for my credit card." Cough. "The lady in front of me was handing her card over, and it dropped to the counter because the clerk had disappeared." Cough. "The gal's loop earrings fell to the counter, turning and spinning, landing on a pile of fake fingernails, false eyelashes, and a nose stud. The lady behind me said she wasn't waiting and left the store without paying."

"Mom, I keep hearing about all these weird happenings, too—it's all over the Internet. I have no idea what to believe." I tell her about the disappearance of John's dead body, then remember the two girls on the swing set, the abandoned bicycle, and the dog with no owner. People are missing.

Mom starts coughing again, but it sounds clearer; no doubt, her air passage has opened. She changes the conversation back to the children and Silvia and Tom's emotional turmoil. She tells me again about Silvia finding their beds empty, then adds, "Dad and I were talking to Gilda next door before we called you. Her granddaughter also vanished. She is only a month old. Marion was nursing the infant, and there, right in mama's arms, the child disappeared, leaving her onesie and a soggy diaper on her lap. I can't imagine such a thing."

I shake my head. What would I do if that happened to Denny and me with our baby? How would we manage the grief? How would you deal with it if you are a parent? A flash of Mark and Melissa's Matty passes my memory. I see the faces of Jack and Jasmine in my mind's eye, yet I don't know them intimately; I've never held them.

"That's horrible, Mom" are the only words I can offer.

"Have you turned on the news yet, Sar?" Her voice is no longer raspy. "It's on every channel except for cartoons. Worldwide events, everywhere from New York, Seattle, and London to Hong Kong, Moscow, and Dubai. Our president is supposed to give a speech soon. What has happened? Will it happen again?"

"Don't ask me. But on the QT, Carl got a report that it could be a new virus that eats away at your body instantly. Might make sense. It happened so fast; hopefully, no pain was involved. But is it contagious? Will or when will it happen again? And why them and not us?"

"A virus? That certainly seems logical. Wait a second. Let me tell Dad and see what he thinks." I hear Daddy talking to Mom in the background, quizzing her about various aspects of the virus theory. Being a self-employed mechanical engineer, he will examine the idea methodically. He deals with problems better than my mother.

"Your father thinks the virus idea makes sense. But couldn't we, here in the United States, have better precautions in place to avoid such a pandemic entering our country again? And he asks how it could happen at the same time everywhere, like instantaneously."

"Don't know, Mom. I don't have a scientific mind like the two of you. Carl is convinced that they'll figure it out. Everything will make sense after things settle down. Tell me, did you happen to hear a sound of some kind before it happened?"

"Why, yes. It was a sound I've never heard before."

"Same here. Maybe that has something to do with it."

There's another pause as I hear her conversing with Daddy and his responding in the background.

"Dad heard the sound, too. He was working in the basement. He didn't know anything was different until I came home and told him about my shopping experience. He wants to know what to do about the people missing. It may be insensitive for us to even discuss it right now, but we ponder what the insurance companies will do. You know—no body, no proof without a death certificate, and no payout. Like when a natural disaster hits and people die or can't be found for months, how do you claim the missing bodies?" Her voice is back to normal; I'm thankful it wasn't a full-blown asthma attack.

Before I can respond, my father is talking again, and Mom starts parroting his words. "Daddy wonders how to oversee the banks, mortgages, credit card payments, you know, regular monthly bills. If these people are gone, won't that bankrupt the United States and perhaps the rest of the world? Will there be a run on the banks for our money? Will it be worse than the recent recession? Will inflation get worse? How will our president, our government, handle everything?"

"Good point," I interject, finally getting in a couple of words. "I'll ask Zoey when I get a chance. I'm sure she'll have information about the banks. But we've no clue how many have disappeared or what percentage of the population is missing. Also, what if they reappear? Will everything go back to normal?

"But back to the topic," I continue, "there are also people with pensions and auto loans and leases to manage somehow if they are gone. If I disappeared and didn't pay my mortgage, what would happen to our townhouse? Who would get it? Who'd pay back our student loans? Would all debt revert to the next of kin? Yeah, let me run it past Zoey."

We talk about Silvia again and mention the time is late in Florida, so I shouldn't call her until the morning. I wouldn't know what to say or how to comfort her right now, anyway.

"What does Denny think about all this?" Mom asks.

My eyes open wide in unbelief. I haven't thought about him in the last several minutes. Is he still mad at me? Surely, he should be back by now.

"I can't find him and haven't heard from him. I think he may have gone out to the plane crash, but he didn't take his phone, and his car is still in the garage. I've been too busy to think about what's happened to him with all that's been going on here." My voice cracks—and not only because of the uncertainty of my financial future without him. Yes, it's a real concern, I wonder: If Denny is gone, will I be able to survive? Will I be allowed to stay here in my home?

"Hold on a sec," Mom says hurriedly.

There's a long pause.

"Did you feel that?" I'm unsure if she's talking to Daddy or me. "Wait."

Do you hear those noises in the background?

The phone stays silent for about ten seconds. Finally, I ask desperately, "What's going on there, Mom?"

"It's okay; we're okay. We're having an earthquake, here in Springfield, of all places. It isn't too strong, but it's still rolling under our feet. Oregon rarely gets them. I hope the epicenter wasn't anywhere near the Cascadia subduction zone. That one is to be a troublemaker someday." With Mom being a professor of oceanography and having a passion for studying plate tectonics, she knows more than I do about earth sciences.

There's a break in the conversation, then she speaks. "Let me check the kitchen to make sure nothing broke."

"Okay, Mom. It's great that you're okay." Relieved my parents are all right, I tell her I must get going, adding, "I need to find Denny soon. I'm getting worried."

I want my husband. I want life to be regular again. Today has been horrible. The cramps are coming back; I should take another Motrin or two.

"He'll show up, Honey, don't worry. He can't be one of the missing, and neither are my grandbabies; I know it in my heart. They can't be. They'll all come back." She tries to comfort me, but we both feel no relief.

A "hope so" is all I can say without starting to cry.

"Don't worry. Daddy and I are thinking of Denny and you. It'll work out; it always does somehow. Let me know when you hear from him. Otherwise, I'll call in the morning. I'll let you go, and make sure you watch our president; he's getting ready to speak now."

"I will. Thanks, Mom. Hugs to Daddy. Glad you're both safe and your asthma didn't cause a problem. And we'll talk to Silvia and you both later. We love you." I hang up the phone with an empty feeling in my head, heart, and stomach.

Good grief—earthquakes now? I'm trying hard to remain calm. I'm caught up in the moment of all these missing people, but what's coming next?

Are you hanging in there, too?

~ Silvia ~

The president and politics—oh, how I dread those two topics. Could you tell I've avoided those subjects since you entered my mind? I don't like going there. Yes, there's turmoil in America, with the far right and the far left and the hatred between the two parties and our president. I get that, and I try to stay neutral. But with other countries like Russia, China, Iran, and Israel having ongoing issues, it makes me question why we can't get along. Are you a stubborn Trump conspirator or a virtue-signaling liberal progressive? I won't judge you; I won't even tell you which party I prefer. I only wish we would stop all the bickering and learn to live together.

We both could give our perspectives on America's economy, sky-rocketing inflation, gas prices, power-grid breakdowns, broken food chains, and environmental catastrophes that could be due to any number of factors, but why bother? Enough already.

What we need is someone strong who can quickly and effortlessly draw both sides to the center and implement sensible policies, not only for here in the States but also for the entire planet. Someone who could stop these nonsensical wars and invasions of countries. Someone. Please. No more fighting.

I'm weary of it. Please admit it, so are you. We need a savior, someone who can turn this all around. Right now.

After disconnecting the call, I tap my phone to life again. I have an idea: Maybe Mark has heard from Denny. I don't have him on autodial, but I remember calling him a couple of weeks ago; I search in my phone's database for a 602 Arizona area code. Pressing the recall number, I wait to hear Mark's ebullient voice. His machine answers with a perky greeting, saying he'd love to take my call, but he's out of the office, and that I should please text or email him my order. That's the Mark we know and love, always the happy, helpful salesman, even if he has found a new religion.

I wait for the beep and start my message. "Hey, Mark. Have you heard from Denny? Thought he may have talked to you recently. Please let me know. Hugs to Melissa. Oh, this is Sarah."

After swiping the "Disconnect" button, I recheck my calls. Since I already talked to Mom, I erase her message without listening to what's undoubtedly a disheartening report.

I review Zoey's terse text about having been stood up and reply: *Where R U now? All OK? Call me!* I must ask her about our finances, especially if the economy might collapse. And yes, she'll need to tell me about her latest dating disaster.

Within seconds, I get a return text from her: *I'm fair. Idiots everywhere. Stuck in traffic. Will stop by when home.*

Looking forward to it is my reply.

I send Silvia a quick text that I hope she doesn't get until morning, mentioning how sorry I am to hear about the kids being missing.

I don't know how you feel right now, but I'm not in the mood to speak to any other human being for the rest of the day unless it's Denny.

What a crazy day.

I'm drained both physically and mentally. Could the meds be wearing off already and fatigue is starting to envelop me? I turn my phone's screen off and stick it in my pants pocket in case my husband happens to call.

After heading for the couch in our living area, I pick up the remote control for the flat-screen television hanging above the fireplace and click it on. Even though Alexa's remains are strewn on the hearth, at this second, I'm too tired to clean her up—I need a shut-down-and-regroup break. My energy is spent. But at least I'm not in any physical pain. Emotional pain is another matter. This day can't get any worse. Although I tell myself I'm still in control, I feel like a train wreck.

What do you think is going on here?

At least I know you're not missing, too.

Got any answers or theories for me? How do you interpret all this?

I prop the heels of both my bare feet on the glass coffee table's wrought iron legs in front of me.

Let's get our president's viewpoint.

The news station appears with the background of the same flashing photos I saw on the Internet. A newscaster says they're interrupting their coverage for a statement by the president of the United States.

The television revives my almost-spent attention.

"Good evening, fellow Americans. I have a brief statement to make."

Do you think our leader looks pensive with those steely blue eyes staring at the camera? I'm sure he is trying not to falter or break down. It must be a hard speech to give so quickly after what's happened.

When he starts speaking, it's obvious he's reading a teleprompter, as his eyes slowly move back and forth, barely blinking:

> Due to the unusual events of less than two hours ago, it's my duty to inform you, the citizens of the United States and the world, of the status of our country, our earth. As many of you know from watching the news, searching on the Internet, and listening to the radio, across the nation and throughout the world, many of our family members and friends recently inexplicably vanished. Like each one of you, my wife and I mourn our loved ones who have disappeared. We all hope and wish they will somehow be in touch or show up on our doorsteps momentarily.

His words are said in a monotone, lacking excitement and tranquility.

> Right now, all of us feel deep pain. We already are grieving for our missing young children and babies, innocent and with little understanding. We lament the twelve hundred plus who may have lost their lives in three major airline accidents which occurred within minutes of each other, and we mourn the

> lives of our loved ones tragically claimed in auto, boat, bus, plane, or train accidents around the globe.
>
> We don't know yet how many are missing, only that the numbers may be chillingly high. My family and I have close relatives counted among them, including our precious grandchildren; we know the pain, loss, fear, and heartbreak that you are, no doubt, feeling as well.

You can see by his rigid demeanor how hard he is trying to stay stoic and calm. I bet if I had to make this speech, I would be weeping right now, would you?

> I regret to say that so far, with quick research, every country, state, city, town, community, and family everywhere may have somehow been affected by this phenomenon. European, Asian, African, North and South American, and Australian countries have been reporting these tragedies. It seems that there's not one human on earth, our blessed planet, untouched by this catastrophe.

He pulls out a handkerchief and dabs his eyes. Then he takes a sip of water and continues.

> As of this minute, top scientists and all national security agencies, as well as state, county, and local government personnel from across the U.S. and other countries, will be concentrating their collective resources around the clock to find out

> why this has happened, what can be done to prevent it from happening again, and how we can go about bringing back those who are missing. Clothing, articles, and personal belongings they've left behind will be examined and scrutinized.
>
> Already we tend to believe that a deadly virus or type of biological, chemical, or organic compound or even weapon is the culprit. We are considering that the strange sound heard at the same time around the world might have triggered a chain reaction, causing many to disappear. Unlike our lengthy battle against COVID and its variants, we're hopeful this could be a one-time occurrence. We're also praying that there's a scientific solution to bring all missing persons back from wherever they went.

The camera zooms in for a close-up as the president pauses and looks directly into its lens.

> Don't fear; the mystery can and will be solved as soon as possible. It's my—it's *our*—top priority.
>
> During this international crisis, we should take every opportunity to step forward with the other nations of the world and join in peace—a peace like none other, bonded by the loss of our loved ones who could be missing. We now must learn to live, love, and rebuild together through our grief.

> In two weeks, the Omnilateral Commission and the European Council have been planning to meet in Rome to discuss mankind's economic and ecologic future. It's my understanding that, instead, they will be focusing solely on this current aberration, seeking answers and helping us deal with its immediate and long-term problems. We've dealt with disasters of this type before, from deadly hurricanes, tornadoes, flooding, and forest fires to Zika and Swine flu, SARS, Ebola, COVID, and monkeypox; we know we can overcome such catastrophes. At this important meeting, we will work together to figure out the next steps for guiding us and our world through these trying times.

His voice is getting hoarse; he stops to take another sip of water.

> Also, I was just informed there have been two high-magnitude earthquakes in downtown Seattle, Washington, minutes apart. Our thoughts are with those involved as we hope the damage to life and land is minimal. It's my understanding that communication in this region is completely offline as they deal with the crisis and its aftermath. So far, there are no indications that the quakes have caused any tsunamis like the collapsed glacier did last week, destroying a small Alaskan town. Scientists are also tracking the Pacific Northwest's twenty major volcanoes in the Cascade Arc, as there has been a

> substantial increase in recent activity at several of them.
>
> We have a lot of work cut out ahead of us regarding the why and how of this problem and are committed to finding answers. But as of right now, we do not know—it is too soon; we simply do not have enough information.
>
> In closing, I encourage you to share your grief openly with one another, deal with the pain respectfully, and help and give comfort to those around you. Be positive and pray that our loved ones will be returning shortly. Remember the wise saying that "There is a season for everything." Put any sorrow and frustration away, especially toward your brothers and sisters here and everywhere. Use this incident as a pivotal point to unify us as a genuine one-world order. Face the new dawn with promise. Our thoughts and blessings are with you and yours, and I'll keep you, the people, informed of our progress. Thank you and good night.

With his brief speech ended and no opportunity for questions and answers, the commentaries begin: Reporters and talking heads search each phrase and nuance for hidden meanings, possible scenarios, and the promotion of personal and political ideology. Of course, I expect both political parties to volley the rights and wrongs of words spoken, arguing about whose agendas are being followed and whose are ignored. This is standard; this is how it always happens in the news. And I'm sure you know how it works, too. This is only one of the reasons I don't do politics.

I click off the television and watch the screen fade to black. Wondering if my parents felt the second quake, I send them a quick text, hoping for an instant reply, but I know communication services could be jammed or down in their area. I push my fears of them being injured or dead to the back of my mind, reminding myself that they're hundreds of miles south of Seattle.

Good, something productive will come out of all that has happened. I know it, and I feel it. The president is right: The world may reach peace over such a strange occurrence. I only hope that what's happened isn't repeated, causing more people to disappear. We will remember our loss, pick up the pieces, and promote peace. We must make a better world for our children and ourselves. Families will be together again; we will grow and become one people. Whatever has happened or will happen, we can make here, where we live, a better place. Someone will explain it to us; someone will have all the answers and guide us through recovery from this apparent disaster.

Do you feel the same way about it?

And I bet you a hundred dollars that, years from now, scientists will find it was, indeed, the strange sound that triggered it all—a sound like an audio superbug that launched some once-in-a-lifetime virus or chemical reaction infecting only specific, especially weak, individuals. The young and old were affected, and we strong ones were left to change and improve where and how we live. There's a reason that all of this has happened.

Mark my words, we are the champions of the world. The strong survived this cataclysmic event, and we who didn't succumb to the sound have the duty, the obligation, to make this world, our world, a better place.

What a perfect opportunity to turn a nightmare into a utopia!

Don't you get it?

I—you—*we* are in control.

Two chirps on my smartphone snap me out of my pragmatic thoughts. The first is Mom dual texting Silvia and me, stating *We're OK!* I immediately text back, thanking her for the report and saying I'm relieved her message went through. The second one is from Silvia, asking me if it's okay to call.

Within seconds, my sister's number is pushed on my speed dialer. Knowing it will probably be a trying conversation, I keep myself occupied by seeing if Alexa can be reassembled.

"Sil? How are you doing?" I ask as I assess her voice for her emotional status.

"I'm a total wreck, Sar. I don't know—what to do—right—now." My poor sister gags through her sobs and cries. "I'm not sure if I should go someplace or talk to someone about filing a report. Should I sit here on the floor of our family room amongst all the toys and wait for my babies to reappear? And did you hear about the two quakes near Mom and Dad? I hope they're alright."

Isn't it heartbreaking to hear the sorrow in her voice?

"Yes, did you see the text they just sent? They're okay. I'm sorry about Jack and Jasmine, Silvia. How heartbreaking. We'll get answers soon, I hope. How is Tom doing? Is he okay?"

"He left about fifteen minutes ago, right after we heard what sounded like a nearby explosion. Apparently, the warehouse alarm went off, so he went to check it out."

Tom and Silvia live near Orlando, and his construction business is in a commercial area less than a mile from Disney World in Lake Buena Vista.

"Hold a sec. He's texting me on the company phone."

I wait, hoping it's nothing more than a false alarm of some sort. Don't you hate it when your day is atrocious and ruined, one that you'll never forget for the rest of your life, and then a minor incident adds to the pile of problems? I notice my anxiety is going up again; is yours? Please, Sarah, keep calm for your sister's sake.

Silvia comes back to the phone, gasping, "What's going on today? A bomb exploded at Disney World. Tom heard it on the news driving to the warehouse—that was the explosion we heard! Why now? Why here? Why after everything else has happened?"

"Yikes, Sil. That's crazy! Was anyone injured or killed?"

Silence.

I try another angle, "Sis, was this explosion the only strange sound you heard today?"

"No, we heard a different sound right before the kids vanished."

For several minutes, I try to calm both of us down by theorizing that the disappearance and explosion are entirely separate and unrelated incidents. She hadn't heard the president's speech or considered the strange sound to be related to people disappearing. As I collect the shattered pieces of Alexa, I suggest the blast may have been an accident when a driverless car crashed into something, or maybe it was a freak of nature.

"I just turned the television on to a local station," Silvia reacts, "and authorities are already calling it another terrorist bombing. Great. This world is hopeless. People are pure evil. Why are people so sick? I hate what we've become. Are we headed for a civil war? Where are love, peace, and humanity that balance and center our universe? Oh, Mother Earth, rescue us." She mumbles something about karma and how her inner spiritualism is the only basis for existence, but her voice quavers with uncertainty. She cries again when she mentions her babies. I don't know how to comfort her, do you?

"Tom texted me again," she continues, harnessing her emotions once more. "Looks like a gang is growing out on the street in front of the warehouse, starting to burn trash in the big dumpsters. He says it may escalate to a riot, so will hunker down inside the office until things calm down. To top it off, another huge hurricane is headed toward us tomorrow night. But who knows, maybe it'll keep these wacko people from causing problems."

Can you believe this? No one is safe; no one is in control. It's disgusting, isn't it?

Do you feel my stress ramping up again? How much more can I take—can you take?

I do my best to say the right things to comfort my sister and her growing problems, but my words seem meaningless. With little left to talk about, we say our love yous and goodbyes, both wishing for a safe and better tomorrow.

After tossing the broken pieces of the smashed Alexa into the trash compactor, I press a button on the refrigerator and request a digital assistant replacement to be shipped to our address. I engage the unit again, "Alexa, what's the hurricane update in Florida?" When she responds that voluntary evacuation orders are in place and recommends being careful, my fear for Silvia and her family skyrockets.

I must regroup. I must be cool and collected. I must. You should too.

If only the bad parts and tragic memories of our lives could be tossed in the garbage and replaced like new.

~ Aunt Amy ~

I'm worn out, aren't you? I want to crash and forget today's constant turmoil but must forge onward. Somehow, my adrenaline is keeping me intact although my heart is in pieces. And still, Denny has not walked back into the house. At this point, I feel I have no strength to get angry, cry, or even care. Right now, he should be ashamed for not contacting me.

To reroute my attention, I get a stemless glass from the cupboard and pour myself wine from the bottle of shiraz I opened earlier. I take an ample gulp for starters, figuring the alcohol will numb my senses. While in the kitchen, I look out the window and see about fifty people hanging around the access road near the field. I continue to tell myself Denny's among them.

The "Sorry" email from Aunt Amy piques my interest. May as well keep busy and open her email as I dilute my anxiety with an adult beverage. Probably another dissertation about my wicked ways and how I must become a holy roller like she is. I'll only do a quick read; I have no time for her propaganda.

In reopening my email server, I notice the time she sent me her missive: right when Denny and I were eating dinner, arguing, which was about thirty minutes after she left. Since she lives off Sepulveda Boulevard, about ten minutes away, it must be important if she emailed that soon after she arrived home.

I click the "Open" tab while I take another swallow of wine and start reading:

Sarah,

I write this email with a heavy heart. I've been working on the words for several days and decided to send this now since I stopped by a few minutes ago, and we had another confrontation.

In redoing my will, it got me thinking about when I'm no longer around. Although I know beyond a shadow of a doubt that after my death I'll be in Heaven, you, my lovely niece-in-law, keep coming into my thoughts.

I must get it off my chest. I need to apologize to you, right now. I'm sorry, so sorry for how I've behaved these past years of your marriage. I'm wrong. I've done wrong to you. I'm sorry when I'm sharp or terse with my words.

Well, I muse, this is a good start to her email. I'll give her credit for heading in the right direction for once. Interesting it took her days to write—what's up with that? As I take another drink, I ask you what you think of her, yet you don't reply.

Remember when we first met at lunch with Denny? I was so pleased to meet you finally and proud Denny found someone special. I was nervous that day, especially since I'd never been through one of the boys having a serious girlfriend, let alone later marrying them. I didn't and still don't know how to act as your aunt-in-law. Denny was and is so in love with you. You're beautiful, smart, and well-educated. To be honest, you intimidated me from the get-go, and even more so when Denny and you got engaged and married.

My mind floats back to our engagement. Lifeguard Station Number 17 at the Santa Monica Pier with a bottle of champagne at sunset. Truly romantic, with Denny on bent knee, promising his love to me with that gorgeous diamond ring he designed. Later that evening, we stopped by and told Amy. She seemed to be happy for us, but she was hard to read. In retrospect, she might have been forcing that smile of hers.

Sarah, I need to apologize to you for so many things. I distinctly remember carrying on and on about the end times, what we call the Rapture, when we Christians are taken from the earth in the blink of an eye. I shouldn't have blabbered; I apologize if I made you feel uncomfortable about the topic. I didn't realize at the time you wanted nothing to do with my beliefs. I tend to be forceful in my ways, not allowing you to have your own. Do forgive me, please. I didn't and never want to be a stumbling block to you.

Yeah, I remember that and all the other instances, Amy, when you'd try to nail me with your religion. I think back to other emails and letters she's sent me. Most included Bible verses; some of the snail-mailed letters had Bible tracts, which, of course, I discarded immediately.

Sarah, I also want to apologize for continually insisting you believe what I believe. I don't mean to, but somehow it comes out, and I say the wrong things at the wrong time, making a bigger wedge between us—between you and me, between Denny and me, and maybe, sometimes, between you and Denny. I should be patient and kind, but I'm far from it and need work in that area. I think I can somehow bully or shame you into receiving Christ, but I can't. Only the Holy Spirit knows each of our hearts, and all things are in His timing. I know I should lighten up and let Him work in you, but I keep messing things up. Yes, God has plenty of work still to do in me.

I don't want the divide to get wider between us; I want us to be friends, to love each other. I don't want you to hate me. I want so much to be a part of your lives, yet I feel lost and unsure when I'm around both of you, or when I say something that you perceive as stupid, or it is! I apologize for my big mouth. I want to love you and you to love me, but I feel we can't win for trying. With every step forward, we take two steps backward. I can't help but think about a greater love—God's love. Do you know He loves you more than Denny or I possibly can? He loves you, Sarah.

Great, here she's approaching her pulpit. These are kind words, but this lady will never get it, will she? Surely you have someone in your life like her. What do you do to get that person off your back?

I feel burdened to write one Bible verse here about love. Only one, I promise. "But God commendeth His love toward us, in that, while we were yet sinners, Christ died for us." It's a simple verse, but it means so much to me. God loves you, Sarah, more than we can ever fathom. And Jesus Christ died on the cross for your sins and mine, blotting them out forever. And then He rose from the dead, to prove that His Father had accepted His sacrifice on our behalf. That's all—that's all you must believe to have peace with Him and spend eternity in Heaven.

You know me, I want to be like God and love you as He does. I know I can't reach such a love, but I want you to know what's in my heart. I want you to forget how I've behaved in the past. Please help me mend the gap in our relationship. Please forgive me for my past errors and try to forget when I've lashed out at you. I'm sorry for those lashings, for my preaching at you, and for all the times I've admonished you. I should not be saying these things to you.

Oh, Sarah, please, please forgive me for not being sensitive and being so demanding. Please.

My eyes race through the email, wanting to skip through the religion and savor her apologies.

I promise I'll try to keep my mouth shut and not preach at you or Denny, although I know he believes in Christ, and you don't want any part of it. I'm aware of what you think. Now I need to show you my sincerity with actions, not with my words—that's where I've been wrong all these years.

I want only to encourage you to think about God, but I don't want to do it with force. And if you think you're not good enough to be one of His children, please realize that everyone falls short of His glory, but He loves you; He really loves you.

From now on, I want the Holy Spirit to guide me concerning how to approach you. Yes, I'll continue to pray for you daily, but I'm worried about your life in the hereafter. I'll start today to do my best not to harangue you about these things.

Time is short, Sarah. No one knows what tomorrow brings, and that's why I feel compelled to send this email now—to tell you now, this minute in time, that I love you, and I'm sorry. Will you please forgive me, and let's start fresh?

All my love,,
Amy

WELL, THAT WAS STRANGE. Heartfelt and different coming from her. Glad she came to my point of view. I hope she stops her perpetual proselytizing. Wonder if she will. Well, I have it in writing, so can always email it back to her the next time she gets on my nerves.

I am so sick of hearing about her religion. You can take all the Bible verses and shove them out the window from the tallest building and let their tiny, unimportant words flitter slowly to the ground. Nice try, but no thanks. I've made peace with who I am, even if strange things are happening all around me. She must learn that I am me, and I'm not changing. Do you feel the same way about the whole God/Jesus topic?

I shut down the email program and finish my wine. Closing my laptop cover, I realize I never cleaned the lasagna pan. I feel that if I keep busy, I won't have to deal with anything, including the last two hours of horrible tragedies and my husband's disappearing act.

After removing the water-logged burnt cheese with the pot scrubber, I put the pan in the dishwasher along with James's and my tumblers and place the brush back under the sink.

Do you think I should respond to Amy's email? Am I supposed to reply? Wouldn't you agree her Rapture topic about Christians being taken away was rather timely? Quite a coincidence, her mentioning this right now, in light of today's happenings.

Moving on, what would you do if a relative sent you a letter like this? Would you believe her? Trust her? Stick to your guns? Reply?

Onward.

Time to find my husband. I need him. My head and heart are on overdrive as I fight back the tears. I want to cry, but I'm afraid of letting down my guard. I never want to look or feel powerless, yet my outward phlegmatic demeanor is cracking. Denny's the only person who may be able to calm me before I go totally out of control.

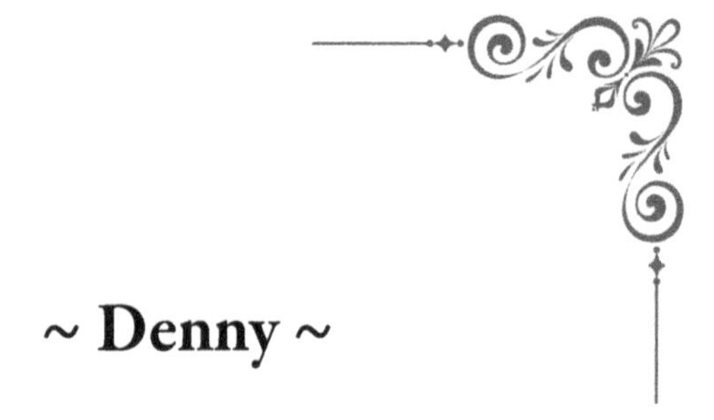

~ Denny ~

Let's start at the beginning. I was in the kitchen washing dishes when you and I heard that crazy noise, and the girls disappeared from the swing set, right? Denny was upstairs, brooding over our lovely squabble.

After seeing no calls or texts on my cell phone, I put it back in my pocket. At the staircase, I grab the banister and head upward. Each step is hardwood like the downstairs flooring, and a turning landing is at the halfway mark. On the second floor, the wood continues to flow down the hall.

His stark white office door remains closed. Do you think he never left?

Well, time for confrontation. Let's get this over with.

Come with me—you can be the middleman in our marital discord.

Whatever I don't want to deal with, now is the time, Sarah. Time to get it over with and get answers. I'll concede that he was right if he's behind this closed door. Anything to restore peace between us amid this chaos.

I put my hand on the door handle. He hates interruptions, but the guy had to have heard all the commotion, even if he happened to be wearing those noise-cancellation headphones he's gaga over.

Turning the doorknob and opening the door, I do a cursory check of the room as I call out his name one more time. The computer screen on his corner desk is blackened, but I can see by the green light that it's powered up. The table light brightly shines down, and the window is half-open, with blinds flittering every few seconds in the mild breeze.

As I had somehow known in my heart: There is no Denny.

Did you expect the same?

The back of his oversized executive leather chair faces me, and the headphone cord hangs from it to the nearby sound system.

Odd. Denny would never leave his headphones all catty-rumpled like that. Not at five hundred dollars a pop dealer cost. He'd protect those babies during any calamity.

I approach the chair and swivel it around.

No!

No.

No, I cry. This can't be!

Oh, my. No!

Denny's long-sleeved dress shirt slips off the chair to the floor. I notice his gray slacks are on the rug with his shoes and argyle socks sticking out under them. His striped boxer shorts are placed perfectly inside the pants.

No. Denny can't be one of them. He can't be missing!

His watch is visible halfway under the desk's file cabinet where he keeps his commission reports. It is still latched.

The business phone rests on the edge of the desk with a red light blinking.

A highlight marker lies on the floor, pointing to the flow charts scattered a couple of feet away.

The headphones remain lodged between one of the chair's armrests and the seat cushion.

No, this can't be happening!

I fall to my knees near his chair. Where did he go? Why did he go? Did the sound affect him, too? Did he get this virus? Will he ever return?

Tears are running down my face as I stretch my hands out on a small rug that rests under the office chair. I wail.

No!

Not my Denny!

Then I spot an opaque object. I rub my fingers through the rug's fibers; I retrieve it, examining it carefully. It looks like part of a porcelain dental crown. Could it be Denny's?

While I'm on my knees, I notice something else on the floor under the green wing chair—over there—near the bookcase where he keeps his factory price books.

Crawling on all fours to the spot, I lie down flat on my stomach and reach around a side table to the chair's back leg that's against the wall.

There.

His ring, Denny's wedding ring. Our ring.

It must have bounced or rolled over here.

The beautiful ring he designed with engravings to match mine.

The white gold band is placed on my first finger, and I fall into one of the wing chairs.

I cry. *My Denny, my Denny, why?*

This can't be real—it must be a dream. Wake me up from this nightmare. I don't want to be here anymore. Please help me.

From across the room, I survey his desk. My eyes go back and forth from the connector of the headphones into the sound system, down the coiled cord to their landing on the chair.

A green button is on the headphones. It must be in the "Play" mode.

Dennis was listening to something while he worked. Probably that new digitally remastered John Lennon album he downloaded last night.

The music must still be playing. A nice feature on some sound equipment—unlimited music until one hits the "Off" button.

I bet the song "Imagine" will be on; it's Denny's all-time favorite.

Swiveling the chair around, I don the headphones and sit down.

A contact lens, face-up on the keyboard's letter "J," catches my attention as noise starts to flow into my head.

There's talking.

Talking?

What? Not music? Not Lennon's view of universal peace?

The sound is clear and calm. A man is talking in a quiet voice.

> ... the Bible says *that if thou shalt confess with thy mouth the Lord Jesus, and shalt believe in thine heart that God hath raised Him from the dead, thou shalt be saved ...*

What, Denny was listening to God-talk? No way. I am so astonished that I don't hear the guy at first.

> *... for the same Lord over all is rich unto all that call upon him. For whosoever shall call upon the name of the Lord shall be saved.*

Right, Denny? Sure, he must have called on God and was saved all right—ha. So saved he no longer exists here on earth and was taken away, "raptured," as Amy would declare.

No more, no more of this stupid religion!

Standing up, I rip off Denny's prized possession, one he no longer can enjoy now that he's vanished. I throw the phones violently against the wall. They hit the framed photo of him and John standing at the eighteenth tee box at Pebble Beach. The picture's glass shatters and falls to the floor.

I scream profanities at the walls as anger seethes inside me.

"Denny!" I cuss as I fall to my knees, repeatedly pounding the rug with closed fists.

I pull myself into the fetal position. I am out of my mind. I don't care what you are thinking or who you are right now as you see my meltdown. I'm not ashamed of my actions or my words. I'm past the point of being rational. I let out the loudest scream I can, hurting my ears and my brain—no doubt the vicious roar pains you, too.

I search my soul, wondering why Denny is gone and I am not.

Denny was taken away, yet here I am, alone and brokenhearted. Was there something about him that the sound affected? Was he a weak person who didn't have some anti-disintegration survival gene that I have?

Or could Aunt Amy possibly be right? Was he raptured?

I feel out of control. There's nowhere to turn.

~ Alone ~

I don't know how long I've been lying on the office floor, and I don't care. It could have been minutes, hours, or days. Does it matter?

What should I do?

Denny has left me.

Why? Why did he leave?

Who else left me? Did you? Are you here with me? Why do I bother asking you? You've been of no help since we started this relationship. You're of no value to me; you can't help me in any way, shape, or form. Yes, I'm lashing out at you, you who can ignore me or leave me at any moment—who can walk away and be done with me. Relationship over and ended. At this second, I hate you. I hate that you have the choice of turning away and forgetting I exist.

Go ahead. Shut down the AI program. Close the book on me and put it on a shelf to collect dust forever. Walk away from me.

But remember this, I'm stuck here, alone.

Feeling like my head is going to explode with fury at Denny, the world, you, and this alleged God, I get up and stumble into the hall.

Moonlight is filtering in from the skylight above. I hear sirens outside, along with muffled laments from neighbors coming to grips with the fact that their loved ones are among the missing.

I am desperately lonely; I beg you to respond. Do you hear the alarms and wailing, too? Do you have any idea how many of your loved ones are gone? Please, please answer me. Say something, anything!

But you stay silent, so I'll stop speaking to you and try to stop you from invading my thoughts. For now, I'm done with you. Call me self-absorbed—call me pathetic—call me anything you want. I don't want you here in my head anymore. Go away, find someone else to bother, to watch everything they do or say or feel. Leave me.

I rub my eyes, trying to make you, the pain, and the sorrow go away. Barrenness is within me. Broken and trounced.

I retreat to our bedroom. I feel despondent. To think of the weeks I've spent choosing every element in this room, from the four-poster bed to the elaborately carved dressers. In this condo, for that matter, it all seems meaningless now. Denny hadn't been all that interested in my finds; if only I'd spent that time on him instead of decorating this place, maybe he'd still be here.

Staring at our wedding photo on Denny's bureau, I pick it up and examine it for clues about today's defection. It had been a small affair in Malibu, on a bluff overlooking the Pacific Ocean. My parents were there, along with Silvia and Tom, Mark and Melissa, Hal and Aunt Amy, Carl and his wife, and a few friends. My dress was white floor-length chiffon with ribbons flowing down the back, and I was barefoot as I walked on grass flanked by white chairs. Sarah, the barefoot bride—everyone knows I can't stand wearing shoes or socks. The photo shows us standing under a white archway covered with white roses; the sun was setting behind us across the deep blue water. It had been a beautiful ceremony. Afterward, we celebrated at a nearby restaurant, and the next day we flew to Cabo San Lucas for a ten-day, relaxing honeymoon. We were so in love.

Yes, Aunt Amy had come to our wedding and hadn't said one offensive word.

Noticing Denny's wedding band on my hand, I slip it off and set it on top of his dresser. No need to wear it now; he's gone. Nothing is the same. I have nothing. I am nothing.

Besides, the ring is so loose on my finger I could lose it, and then what if he returns? What are the chances of that happening?

I pull out my smartphone and plug it into the wall charger on top of my dresser, a bedtime routine. I hear nothing outside now. Curious, I peer through the blind slats and try to study the carnage on the access road and field beneath our window, but it is too dark. I only see blackened parts strewn across the area. How many people lost their lives today at the crash? How many are missing or died around the world? The numbers must be staggering.

Depressed, I head for our bathroom and grab a bottle of anti-inflammatories from the medicine cabinet behind the side mirror. I open the cap and look inside.

Should I end it all?

Would a dozen pills be enough to do it?

Denny's gone. I'm alone.

I feel no hope.

There's nothing to live for anymore. Not even a baby, my husband's baby, growing inside me.

I feel empty.

I place three tablets in my mouth, knowing they will do nothing for my broken heart but will at least keep my cramping at bay. Using the palm of my hand to collect the faucet's flowing water, I take a drink and swallow the pills. In putting the medicine back in the cabinet, I spot Denny's bottle of Ativan, an anti-anxiety prescription he had for his dreaded dental work six months ago. He always took one to calm his nerves whenever the dentist drilled away.

I open the plastic bottle and look inside. At least a half dozen are left. I wonder if I take all of these at once, plus more Motrin, will that accomplish the goal? End it all? Kill me, like I wanted to kill the baby who was probably inside me mere hours ago. Would anyone miss me? Would anyone care?

No, I don't have the guts to do something so drastic, so final. I'm too selfish.

There must be more to life after all I've been through today.

I shake a tiny pill into my hand. Only one won't hurt me, but it should calm my nerves and let me sleep. Using no water, I ingest the tablet and return the jar to its place.

Next, I undo the ponytail in my hair, take off my clothes and toss them in the hamper, turn on the shower, and step inside. I'm surrounded by shiny, hand-crafted tiles—more evidence of husband neglect and home-design obsession, I suppose.

While my tears blend with the water cascading over my skin, I wish the hot rinse would wash away my loss and sorrow. But it brings me no relief.

After my legs get tired of standing under the steady stream and my fingers show expanding wrinkles, I turn off the spray, grab an oversized towel, and vigorously wipe my body dry, thinking the rubbing will exorcise the recent memories.

I finish my hygiene routine clinically: brushing the tangles out of my hair, cleaning and flossing my teeth, slathering moisturizer over my face, and tossing the damp towel on the growing pile of laundry.

Padding to the walk-in closet, I pull on a pair of funky, hot-pink sweatpants and a black T-shirt declaring "I Love Israel." Hal sent it to Denny last Christmas; it was too small for him so became mine. Its soft fabric against my skin provides a hint of the comfort I'm desperately craving.

Not wanting to talk, think, or be, I turn off the lights and crawl onto the bed, pushing the six decorative pillows off Denny's side. The bright-blue LED light of the alarm clock tells me it is 9:48 p.m. I stare at it, trying to comprehend how much time has passed since today's fiasco started. I can hear the clock's mechanism as it ticks, ticks, ticks. Time continues with or without me.

Curling up in a tight ball on top of the soft comforter, I toss and turn, wondering if, after I fall asleep, I will wake up from this terrible dream.

My smartphone lights up the room with its screen, alerting me to a new text.

When I retrieve it from the dresser, I see that its message is from Jeremy: *U around? Can't find my parents.*

Me: *Sorry, J. Denny's gone, too.*

Within seconds, Jeremy replies: *Want me to come over?*

I hesitate. How I'd love to be held in someone's arms right now—by anyone who cares for me. What should I do?

Knowing somehow you're still there, I feel your presence within me. You must still want to be here, to continue this journey with me. That means you must care about me. Thanks. It gives me a little solace to know that someone does.

So, tell me: Would you invite Jeremy over? I pause, waiting for your reply, but it never audibly arrives.

You're right. A definite no. I know he has deep feelings for me, but I can't go there right now. At this second, I can't think about a relationship that could be more than friendship. Thanks for reminding me to do the right thing.

I take a deep breath and type: *How sweet. Not this time - took meds to sleep. Wouldn't be good company.*

Within seconds, he replies: *U sure? I would come if U want - just say so. Anytime. I'm here 4 U.*

As nonchalantly as I can, I reply I'm sorry to hear about his parents and will see him at work tomorrow as I have nowhere else to go or do. Although I'm lonely and hurting right now, I refuse to acknowledge any present emotions about Jeremy or his possible feelings for me. I ache too much. I miss Denny.

His response is only the letter *K.*

The phone gets returned to its charger; I return to bed.

More minutes slowly pass. Lying on my back, I stare at the ceiling, rehashing today's events while trying not to dwell on Jeremy's texts.

Why, why is Denny gone? Do you know? Can you tell me? I mull over that odd sound just before the world turned upside down and inside out and caused hundreds or thousands or maybe millions of people to vanish.

I try to recall the actual sound—it was three sounds in one, as if someone were shouting a word while another voice sounded, and a trumpet blared. All were happening at the same time. I'm surprised that no one is repeating it on the news; there must be a recording. Are they afraid that if they replay it, it may make more people disappear?

My feet feel like ice, so I get out of bed and grab a pair of socks from my dresser. A mindless task, since I only have a few pairs to my name. I almost laugh when I pull them on and realize which ones I've chosen. Silvia gave them to me as a joke Christmases ago, knowing how much I detest wearing anything on my toes. These are the ultimate ugly socks—electric purple, with each knitted toe being another bright color and the letters H, A, P, P, and Y displayed on the toes' tips. They're hideous and a major chore to put on or take off, as each toe must be forced into its designated pocket.

For some strange reason, whenever I'm sick or need my feet warmed, I end up wearing these awful things, although I detest them. The problem is my pinky toes bend inward and don't fill the sock's areas where they should go, causing a chunk of excess fabric to overhang. However, this time, the article of clothing is an oasis of calm in the storm of my disjointed emotions. I'm sure you're thinking they look silly on me, but at this point, I don't care what you or anyone thinks. Don't start harping on me, okay? We've been through too much the last several hours.

I crawl into the bed again; this time I snuggle under the comforter and sheets in an attempt to get warm.

It works. I close my eyes and tell myself everything will work out—it always does. I want to be in control again. I will myself to go to sleep.

WHAT SEEMS LIKE MINUTES later, I awake in a sleepy fog. Someone is knocking, pounding on the front door. Confused, I wonder who it could be.

Is that Denny?

Has he come back to me?

Why isn't the doorbell ringing instead?

Do you know who it is?

I hope you didn't wake up, too, but if you did, can you please answer it for me while I sleep?

I glance at our alarm clock; it is after midnight.

The knocking gets louder.

Do you think it could be Jeremy?

In a groggy daze, I get out of bed and head down the hall. When I set off the motion-sensor nightlight near Denny's office door, I see only dark shadows in the empty room. Not wanting to remember the past, I grab the doorknob and quickly pull the door shut, halfway expecting my action to banish the vacancy inside me.

I hurry down the stairs, hoping whoever it is will stop this insistent knocking.

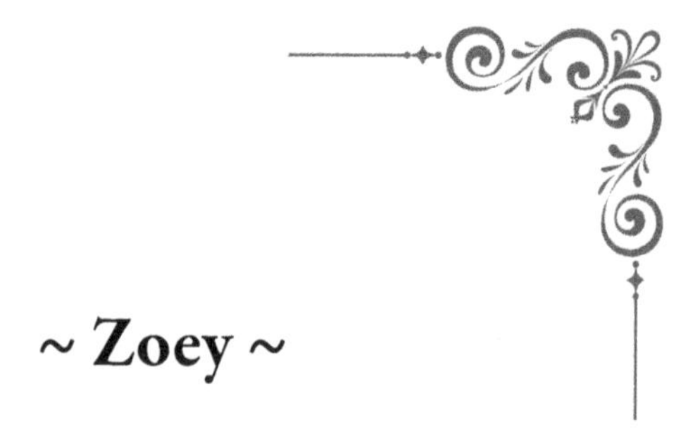

~ Zoey ~

Through the front door's peephole, I see that my visitor is none other than dearest Zoey.

"What are you doing here?" I ask. Upon opening the door, I realize I never set the deadbolt earlier or manually turned on our security system. I was expecting Denny to return, unaware at that point that he was one of those missing. "And why are you here so late? Do you know what time it is?"

"Didn't you get my text? I said I had to come over. So here I am. And after twelve is not *that* late. Where is Denny, and why didn't he answer the door? I must talk to you both, now."

Let me introduce you to my best friend. She's smart, quick-witted, and together. She's one who rarely gets ruffled, although I have to say she appears to be so now. Her black, sleeveless, A-line dress that stops double-digit inches short of her knees accentuates her Middle Eastern beauty. But tonight, she has dark circles under her almond-shaped eyes, and her usually pinned-back, jet-black hair is loose and unkempt.

There's no point in beating around the bush, not with Zoey. "Denny's gone, taken, missing," I tell her. "He is not here." I try to keep fear out of my voice; she doesn't appreciate hysteria.

"Ugh, I wanted you two to do something right away. Now." Typical Zoey. Skip any chit-chat or implications and cut to the chase.

However, I'm not yet ready for that. I am still getting my bearings straight after my brief, medically induced nap. In abbreviated sentences, you hear me tell her about my findings in Denny's office as well as Silvia's missing kids and my parents surviving the earthquakes.

"No way! Denny? Well, that's a shocker. I never thought he'd be missing. Bummer on Jack and Jasmine. Glad your dad and mom are fine." She throws a glance toward the upstairs office door and continues to the kitchen, dropping her briefcase on the countertop and kicking off her four-inch stilettos. "You just never know, do you? Many are gone, and there's no rational reason."

She finally takes a good look at me with her head tilted to one side. "Oh, Sarah, nice rags you're wearing. Did you dress for me? And what is it with those silly-looking socks? I don't think I've ever in my life seen socks that ugly—or, for that matter, you wearing *any* socks. Ever."

You can ignore her digs like I do, as I'm used to her clipped tongue. I disregard her comments, telling her instead about the plane crash and James and his mother.

As I speak, she doesn't respond, but opens the refrigerator and pulls out the Tupperware container of leftover lasagna.

"You don't mind if I eat this, do you? I never got a full meal at dinner tonight, and I'm starving. Boy, date night was pathetic." She picks out a fork from the silverware drawer and digs into the cold food without bothering to put it on a plate or reheat it.

"Perhaps you'd like some wine with your meal?" I ask, miffed that, so far, she has turned a deaf ear to my incredible story about the day's events.

"Yes, please—anything you got, I'm game."

I retrieve the over-half-full bottle I had earlier and pull out two wine glasses from the cabinet above the wine rack. After removing the bottle's rubber cork, I pour us both a healthy drink, leaving about one glass.

Zoey pulls a laptop out of her briefcase and sits on a barstool. Between bites, she rambles, "You must do this; you have to do it before it's too late. It's a shame Denny isn't here; that may complicate things."

Placing her glass of wine on the counter, I grab mine and take a seat on the other chair. "It's a shiraz," I tell her. "Not great but doable for now. We need to finish this one before I open a pinot noir. I know you like something fruitier."

"Fine. Whatever. Now listen to me, Sarah. I'm telling you this in confidence and out of respect for our friendship. What I tell you can't be repeated, got it?" She takes forkful bites of the lasagna between sentences, trying to swallow each one before speaking again. "However, you can tell your folks or sister; just don't name me as your source.

"I'm giving you a heads up. As of 5:00 a.m. E.S.T, American banks are shutting down, with the international ones most likely to follow. There will be a freeze on all transactions. No money in, no money out—until who knows when they can verify that the entire world will not go belly up."

"Really? For sure?" I am flabbergasted. I look into my friend's eyes, knowing that this woman holds a top position at one of the United States' largest banks and has reliable insider information. I completely trust her when it comes to money issues, and so should you.

"Yes, and that means we have less than two hours to protect ourselves." As if in a sudden rush, she packs up the lasagna and returns it to the fridge, then licks her fork and puts it in the dishwasher, thankfully, prongs down.

Holding her laptop in one hand and the wine in the other, she heads for the dining table. "Do you mind if we work over here? That way we can spread out more. And bring your laptop."

Compliantly, I follow her to the dining area, turning on the modern glass lamp hanging over the table. I gather the spread-out photographs and papers from a work project on the pros and cons of the LGBTQ movement and its effect on society, piling them on the far end of the table. We each pull out a white-padded chair and sit down.

"You access your savings and checking accounts online, right?" Zoey is all business. "Including your retirement accounts?"

"Of course, who doesn't these days?" I think of Amy—as you know, she's too fearful of electronics to attempt the feat. I boot up my laptop, click over to our bank's website, and log into our account.

"Okay, first we must tap into your savings accounts and move the money into liquid funds, like checking accounts. This way you'll be able to keep paying your bills if the banks remain closed for more than a few weeks or months."

I nod, pretending I understand but really can't grasp it. I am blown away by the idea of long-term bank lockdowns.

"See, once we move the money out of savings or mutual funds and into a checking account, we can move it again into a more liquid account. That's what I'm doing with my accounts, and I want you to do the same with yours."

Zoey is typing on her computer, whipping through multiple screens at a time, and clicking buttons willy-nilly as she speaks.

"Okay," I agree, opening my first savings account and considering my next click. "I'm with you so far. But won't that mess up my savings and mutual funds?"

"No, we'll leave the minimum amount there, so there won't be any monthly penalties. Do you remember the least amount you can keep without having to pay fees? The average is three to five hundred dollars on standard accounts, but I'm keeping a couple thousand in each of my money-market accounts." She watches my screen as I work, oh so slowly and painstakingly compared to her flying fingers. "That's it. Keep some in savings, but move a decent amount to your checking. You can always move it back when things go back to normal."

"Got it. I understand." I nervously move twenty thousand dollars to checking, leaving three thousand and trusting that this girl knows what she's doing. I click on our travel account and move another four thousand over to checking, again leaving three thousand in the account. I tap on Denny's profit-sharing account with our bank, and it asks for Social Security verification.

"What do I do now, Zoey? They want Denny's info."

"I know it's illegal, and I, in the banking industry, would never say this, but pretend you're Denny—type in whatever lets you get into their system."

I add his memorized nine-digit number, but a rejection notice flashes. I show Zoey the screen.

A slang word pops out of Zoey's mouth. "Looks like they're locking out the retirement accounts already. We better hurry."

My eyes widen as panic sets in. "Then I won't try to touch my IRA. What's next?"

My friend's fingers continue to soar over her keyboard. "Just a second, I'm almost there on my stuff. One more account to do." Zoey is well paid and seems to have plenty of money; I question whether you and I combined have as many accounts as she has. "By any chance, do you or Denny use cryptocurrency—you know, bitcoins?"

"I don't, and I'm not sure about Den. He's always moving money around. Do I need to be concerned about that, too?"

"Just checking. If you don't know, then let's forget about it right now. We could always buy some for backup later if it gets bad. I think online money options will pop up everywhere to keep things going. Of course, all with a hefty fee."

I glance up at the framed oil painting Silvia did in college hanging above the dining-area side of the fireplace. It's a turbulent seascape of waves crashing against coastal rocks with white sea foam showing the ocean's power. When she gave it to me years ago, she said it matched my strong personality that never quits, like the waves. She knows me well. As I've often mentioned, I like to be in control, including of my money.

My short nap plus the drugs must have helped me center back to my normal, logical self. I feel empowered again.

Are there any other bank accounts I should consider? I recall a savings account I've hidden from Denny. I was going to surprise him with a used motorcycle as a birthday present next year—well, that won't happen now, unless he reappears along with everyone else. Perusing the list of accounts, I scroll down to another window and find the funds, moving seven thousand to our checking account.

"Done," Zoey declares triumphantly. "Next, we need to prepay any upcoming bills: mortgages, car payments, and estimated taxes if you or Denny do those. Throw a couple of hundred dollars on your phone, cable, and utility bills, too."

I ask her how many months to pay in advance. "Pay at least one or two; that's all. I'm doing three. This way we won't be on anyone's radar for a while. It'll show you cared enough to circumvent a future problem. No one will be able to take away your house or car keys; they'll hit others before you show up on any past-due report. Hopefully, in a month or two, when everything is normal, you'll be ahead of the curve because you paid in advance."

"What about our student loans?" I hate paying them back but know we're responsible for them.

"Don't bother with those—with everything that's going on, maybe they'll end up being partially paid off as others have recently, even though you two make decent incomes."

"That'd be great."

We simultaneously grab our glasses and take a drink. I click on "Pay Bills" and the "Automatic Pay" section, verifying two months of payments for each bill as I go.

"When you're all done with that," she says, "we need to further liquefy our money. You need a way to get the cash quickly if the banks close long-term, and there's no cash. Credit cards may still be usable; be sure to pay them off completely, so they can be reloaded. But I have a feeling they're going to get maxed out quickly in the next few weeks since so few of us use cash. Plastic is the easy way to go."

"Where'd you find out about this?" I'm sure her info is reliable, but I might feel a tad more comfortable with all this if I knew her source.

After funding our mortgage and two car payments for two months, I cringe when I realize how much money I've spent in a few clicks and then again when I pay off both credit cards that total over four thousand dollars.

She laughs. "One top-level administrator who flirts with me daily called me when I was driving home. I pulled over to a gas station, shut my car off, and talked to him for over a half hour. That and the traffic are why I got here so *late*, as you say. He suggested all this stuff and told me a bunch of interesting things.

"He said that central banks globally have established two ways to handle cryptocurrencies. There is Central Banking Digital Currency, or CBDC, which, instead of print money, uses electronic coins or accounts backed by the full faith and credit of a government. Several countries have already implemented it, and our Federal Reserve has been having open discussions about it. Then, other countries are considering switching to 'payment implants,' you know, like the chip they put in pets for tracking or the medical vaccination identification information. These convenient contactless payment microchips are already implanted in people in Europe and work great, as you no longer have to carry a wallet or purse. It would be a permanent chip in the hand or head that can be accessed easily and always monitored. Using a QR code, like those on products and your smartphone, you simply scan the chip to pay for things when you are in a store or online. Now is the perfect time to do it, with everything that is going on, and either one would be an easy solution to get anything you want without having to think about money. Pretty simple to set up if the banks are closed for a few weeks or months. I'm sure there'll be ample incentives to get the implant to purchase things. But we need to act fast and now, just like he told me."

She stops, takes a breath and sip of wine, and continues. "Next go to PayPal, Stripe, GoCardless, or any of the top online money accounts you use and apply about five hundred dollars to each from your checking account. You may want to do it with Amazon, Target, and even Whole Foods so you'll be able to get tangible goods, although they may be at an exorbitant cost." She turns her attention back to her laptop. I watch her make her arrangements on PayPal and GoCardless. "And don't worry, Sarah, I know these money-transfer sites are tracked by the government for transactions of more than six hundred dollars, but we're staying under the minimum. Down the road, you'll be able to get ahold of this money when needed."

I'm nothing if not obedient in the face of feminine authority. I log onto PayPal and prepare to follow Zoey's orders, wondering if I will have any money left when this is done.

She keeps up her running commentary. "Plus, I doubt the IRS will care about a measly five hundred bucks here and there—we're not moving millions, only trying to survive. With any luck, shipping may not shut down completely, and we'll be able to order groceries, prescriptions, et cetera, online without having to go into a store and deal with people trying to grab it all. Another rumor starting is an intense shortage of food—and

I'm not just talking toilet paper, baby formula, semiconductor chips, diesel fuel, pet food, or eggs. I hope that doesn't happen."

"But what if these companies crash?" I'm sure that is a possibility. We've seen so many businesses go under in the last couple of years.

Zoey barely glances at me. "Well, that could happen, but I doubt the big dogs like Amazon and PayPal will; they're worth too much. I mean, think about it. The Internet may crash too, so all this moving money around may be useless. That's why this cool chip idea needs to start being used right away. But, in the meantime, you can't cover every possibility, and this is how the industry insiders are protecting themselves. We need to do what they do. These are ways to make sure you can get to your money to pay for things over the next few weeks or months before everything goes back online.

"Another option is actual cash. Although banks do not want to keep using it as they move to digital currency, we still should be able to during the transition. Do you keep any at home?"

"No, but I do have my coin collections hidden upstairs."

"Which types of coins?" She asks as she picks up her glass of wine, adding one word at a time between drinks. "Pennies?" Sip. "Nickels?" Sip. "Dimes?" Sip. "Or ...?"

I stop her by rattling off my list, purposely not taking any drinks. "I have almost a complete dime book, a full set of state quarters, Walking Liberty halves, Morgan silver dollars, presidentials, plus some proofs, a few gold coins, and others. My grandfather handed most of it down to me before he died, and I've added to the stash whenever I was in the mood."

She's impressed. "Great! Those are keepers, especially the silver and gold. They should work for a while."

I turn back to my work. I'm not entirely comfortable with her reasoning or with the fact that I have spent so much of our savings, but what do I know? I transfer funds to Amazon, PayPal, and Zelle.

One last click and I'm finished.

"That's it, Zoey. I think I spread it out enough. Thanks for your help. Let's hope it doesn't get as bad as you predict."

"Agreed. But remember how blindsided our grandparents and their parents were when the Great Depression hit. We don't want people going crazy and jumping out of high-rises again."

We both close our computer browsers as she brings up another topic, "I'm sure Denny has life insurance?"

"Yes, a million-dollar policy."

"Unfortunately, you can kiss that goodbye. I can promise you no insurance company is going to be paying off any plan if there's no body."

"My dad was asking about that, too," I add. "Silvia might know for sure, since she works in the insurance business, but considering her children being gone, this is no time to ask her."

"True. But tomorrow, if you can, cancel the life insurance contract," she tells me, as she shuts the lid of her laptop, leaving it closed on the table. "Even if you had a body, they're going to call this a catastrophe, an 'act of God,' and refuse to pay anything. They would all go bankrupt if they had to pay out. That's what I believe."

"You sound so negative, Zoey."

"I'm only trying to protect you. Cancel any life insurance you have on yourself, for that matter. Maybe the insurers will at least refund some of your premiums. Don't procrastinate. Tomorrow is going to be a roller-coaster ride in the finance industry. Pay attention and trust me, girlfriend. Big changes are coming."

With that said, my best friend drains her wine glass and stands. "The last six hours have been a nightmare. Let's finish off that bottle of wine while I tell you about date night."

~ Date ~

I head to the kitchen, retrieve the bottle of shiraz, and pick out a pinot noir from the Willamette Valley in Oregon. My parents sent a case of it down a couple of months ago. It's a delicious wine, and we deserve it after our horrible day. On my way back to Zoey, I select four small, dark-chocolate Dove candies from a glass dish on the fireplace mantel.

You're hanging around, right? I don't mean to ignore you, but you'll find Zoey engaging when it comes to the men in her life.

With a corkscrew, chocolates, my wine glass, and two bottles in my possession, I join my friend in the great room. She has already made herself comfortable on the long couch, bare feet resting on the glass table.

I pour the remaining contents of the bottle of wine into my glass, open the other bottle, explain where it came from, and pour Zoey a drink. My body feels more relaxed; no doubt the meds and alcohol are blending well.

As I fill her glass, she says, "So, let me tell you, girl; no more men for me. No more online dating, either. Ever. Tonight, I met Marco Pattini at Matteo's on Wilshire Boulevard in Westwood. Have you ever been there?"

"Yes, once with Denny, Mark, and Melissa. It's got delicious Italian food, but all those mobs of people crossing the street make it too claustrophobic." I place two of the candies on the table in front of her, adding, "Here, this will make your dating dilemmas go away." I sit on the matching loveseat, tucking my silly-socked feet underneath me, and rest my wine glass and two chocolates on a side table.

"Perfect, choice, Sar! Wine and chocolates make any bad day look better!" She continues with her story without touching the candies. "I don't know about the food—this was my first time at the restaurant, and we never got around to eating. That's how ridiculous tonight was. Anyway, with Marco being Italian, he said it's a good place to go.

"You know me with online dating: I'll research any guy I meet. Marco looked interesting, I thought. He works in telecommunications and has a condominium in Brentwood. He is divorced and has an eight-year-old daughter who I think is demanding, as is his ex-wife; they live in Santa Monica."

She samples the wine, commenting that it's much better than the prior one. I nod in agreement but don't bother to interrupt her. I know you'll be as entertained as I am.

"He walked to the restaurant from where he works. We arrived at the same time and were seated next to a family of six, parents and their four kids. The children were well-behaved and not the bratty type.

"So, he and I are having a decent conversation, talking about our backgrounds, where we grew up, what we do for a living—you know, the easy-breezy details I could give in my sleep I've stated them so often. In the meantime, the server had taken our drink order and delivered two glasses of Chianti along with a basket of warm bread. I started to relax, thinking this guy could have potential, but then his phone rang. He informed me it was his daughter calling, and he had to take it. He excused himself and walked out the restaurant's front door, but I could see him through the door's window standing on the sidewalk, talking on his cell."

That was curious, I thought. "Do you think it was a front so he could ditch you or leave you hanging with the bill?"

"Ha. Seriously, that did cross my mind as it's happened before, Sar. But we hadn't ordered our meal yet. I thought we had chemistry between us. Seconds later, I heard that strange sound everyone is talking about. I looked over at the table with the family. Only the father was sitting there, his face ashen, obviously in shock. His wife and kids had disappeared! Also, the waitress who had served us was filling glasses with water at another nearby table for two, and *poof*, she was gone—ice-cold water spilled all over one of the customers. When another server finally came over to wipe up the mess, she picked up her coworker's clothing from off the floor, complete with her shirt, skirt, shoes, panties, bra, and even what looked like two breast implants. She started sobbing when she carefully collected a gold cross necklace, two bracelets, and a couple of rings by one of the table legs. Meanwhile, I looked out the window repeatedly, but Marco was no longer in view.

"Of course, I had no clue what was going on, so I sat and waited almost an hour for him to return. But he didn't. As everyone was wildly being irrational around me, not only did I eat the bread in front of me, but I also drank both glasses of wine."

Despite the multiple tragedies of today, I laugh. The girl's priorities are food and alcohol. But what else could she do if she expected the guy to return? Would you wait around?

Zoey stares at the ceiling, eyes narrowed like she's picturing the scene. "The restaurant was mayhem; everyone was yelling and confused. Even outside there were crowds of people, so there was no way for me to find this guy. After I'd polished off both glasses, I left two twenties on the table and went to my car. It was obvious Marco was not coming back." She smiles wryly, saying, "We won't be going on a second date, because I believe I was stood up once again."

She sits up and then leans forward, her body language portraying seriousness. "After at least twenty minutes battling the hordes of pedestrians and getting into my car, I hopped onto the 5 into the Valley. Sar, it was twelve lanes of sheer terror. So many accidents or abandoned cars stopped on both sides of the freeway, with drivers doing their best to maneuver around them. I've never seen so many people giving others the finger, never heard such a cacophony of blaring horns. It made no sense. Crazy world! It took me over two hours to drive less than twenty miles. Several times, I was in standstill traffic for up to ten or fifteen minutes. It took me twenty-two minutes to exit an off-ramp to talk to Steve, the guy who gave me the banking tips, and twice as long to drive side streets the rest of the way home.

"Also, I was listening to the radio, and some guy was saying he was at a friend's wake with an open casket. Get this, the dead person's body evaporated right in front of him and everyone there! That would've been spooky."

Not wanting to visualize any ghostly scenarios involving the dead or caskets, I reach for the wine bottle and fill my now-empty glass, asking, "Out of curiosity, did you notice any other children—like when you were walking to your car or driving home?"

She leans over, picks up a Dove, and tops off her wine glass. "Nada."

"That's what I thought. Same thing with newborns, babies, and even the unborn." It's said with a touch of remorse. "They were all taken, along with the adults. Including Denny, I'm afraid. But we were not. What made us different?"

I untuck my legs and stretch them out, wiggling my colorfully socked toes on the edge of the glass table.

"You got me on that one." Zoey unwraps one of her candies.

"Oh, my goodness, girl!" she suddenly cries out.

I practically spill my wine, alarmed at her reaction.

"Did you ever look at those socks, like up close? They spell out "Happy"! Cute, but why are all the letters backward on your left foot but not on the right? How lame is that?" Is she feeling tipsy, or is she merely excited over my socks?

Our laughing feels good. "Sure, I know the writing is backward on the one sock. How else could the letter H be on both big toes?" I wiggle all ten phalanges with flair. "Yes, they look ridiculous."

Shaking her head in mock disbelief, Zoey pops the chocolate in her mouth. She smooths the wrapper so it's flat and shows me its saying.

One of the reasons I buy this brand of chocolates is because each has a saying printed on the inside of its wrapper; my dad and I love reading them so I always have plenty on hand, especially for when he visits next week.

"Ha, this one reads, *Compliment someone.* Well, I already commented about those attractive socks; I could tell you how you may need a mirror to read one of them. But no, here is my compliment: Sarah, my dear friend, this is an excellent wine. I guess we're either celebrating some sort of strange occasion or wallowing in our losses while the world around us has gone amok. Thanks for sharing it with me." She lifts her glass to toast me as she mixes a swig of red wine with dark, rich chocolate.

"Back to reality." She hunkers herself back on the couch. "Then there's your hubby. He's healthy, so why is he gone? Will he come back? If not, will you bother to do a funeral or service or something for him? Is there anything I can do to help?"

"I don't know. My parents are supposed to come next week; they'll help me decide what's best. I can't fathom thinking about all the stuff that needs attention—if he's indeed gone."

"A morose thought. Do you pick out a casket and put it in the ground if there's no body? Or do you put only a marker there instead? It's mind-boggling."

Zoey takes another gulp of wine as we both sit in silence. I've no clue how to answer. I can't even think about tomorrow. Instead, I unwrap one of my candies. "It says, *Call, don't text.* Well, sometimes texting is better, don't you think?" Jeremy and I rarely speak on the phone to each other, preferring to flirt with a cat-and-mouse emotional affair via our keypads.

"I agree." Zoey chuckles. "At least, texting is the way to go when you're ending a relationship. It's quick and efficient—unless, of course," she pauses dramatically, "you'd rather pull a disappearing trick at a restaurant and leave your date hanging."

My friend interrupts my thinking about Denny's nonexistent body and Jeremy's well-defined one.

"I don't want to talk about today's happenings and these missing or taken people," she declares. "Time to change the topic. You texted asking me to call you about something. What's up?"

"Um. It was about finances—as I said, my dad asked about it. Thanks for helping me out." Suddenly I'm feeling fidgety, which could be from the sugary chocolate and alcohol. "It's well after midnight now; the banks are closed. Tomorrow morning I'll text or email and trust the message gets through. I hope they don't run into a cash problem in Oregon."

"They lived through both quakes and are fine." Zoey comforts me. "Their home is paid off, right? I bet they have some cash, food, and extra supplies."

I try to convince myself that if they survived physical shake-ups, they will the financial ones. "Yes, Dad is usually prepared for any disaster. He keeps those emergency kits in the basement with gallon containers of water, medical supplies, and those yucky-tasting MREs or meals-ready-to-eat packets. I'm sure he's got money stashed away, too." I want to be optimistic about this.

"Good." Zoey thinks for a few minutes. "But before that, your first text mentioned needing my wise guidance. You texted right before I got to the restaurant; that's why I didn't have the chance to answer it. Was that about money, too?"

"Oh, I had a problem, but it worked itself out, I hope." I feel silly having to explain myself and consider mentioning Jeremy instead but don't.

"That's a teaser, girl. Tell me. I won't make fun of you, really. Your hideous outfit's fair play, but what was bothering you? Give me something mundane to think about instead of today's troubles."

I almost blurt out my wine, afraid to divulge the secret you and I know, but I'm ashamed to speak aloud about it for the first time.

The room remains noiseless until I exhale loudly. "Okay. I thought I was pregnant today and was considering getting rid of it, you know. I wanted your opinion of the options." I take a drink and add, "But it turned out to be a false alarm, and I'm not or no longer pregnant, so no worries now."

"Seriously? I bet that's a relief. I know you aren't planning to have a kid now. And I fully understand why not. But—well—let me tell you, you may think having an abortion is an easy choice, but it's not. While the entire West Coast may still allow them, there are personal consequences—trust me. The counselors make the decision easy by being flippantly clinical, convincing you it's the 'right thing' to do at the time. But they lie; it haunts you for the rest of your life. Believe me, having had two of them, I can't tell you how I wish I could turn back the clock and make different choices." She pauses and takes another drink.

"Lately, I've been feeling sad about it; I thought about getting counseling again. It sounds melodramatic, but I'll say it: I feel worthless, unwanted, and unloved, and having those children might have made all the difference. I'm having trouble wrapping my head around the truth that I killed my babies voluntarily."

I try to find the words of comfort but cannot. She has always acted strongly on this topic; I never expected such raw honesty. What would you say to her?

She bites her lower lip and continues, "Here we are, years later, and I'm still a basket case, still dealing with it daily, fixated on how old they would be, what they would look like, what they would have been like." She drinks more wine and picks up her second candy, marking the end of the conversation. After opening the package, she sighs and shakes her head. "*Coin a new phrase*. That's a doozy, isn't it?"

I don't respond, only start unwrapping my sweet.

Zoey's expression is something I've never seen before on her face. Is she feeling lost? Or perplexed? Is Ms. In-Charge-of-Everything unsure of herself?

"You mention that these people have been taken," she says solemnly, "yet we haven't been. We're untaken. If all the innocent babies and children are gone, they now may be in a better place. So, are we the unlucky ones left here, the ones unworthy of being taken?

"Here's my phrase, although I am only speaking for myself: I'm untaken; I'm unmissing. Due to my past mistakes and wrong, stupid, selfish choices, I was not taken away like all these others were. I'm the one who blew it. We all did if we're still here; we're all untaken."

I know she's woefully wrong about this. We are good people, she and I, and even you. I make light of her odd comment. "Right, since I'm here with you, I guess I'm proud to be one of the *un-taken* then," I pronounce the syllables slowly and deliberately with noted sarcasm.

However, my words fall flat.

I don't know if the wine has made her lugubrious, if she drank too much, or if she is simply worn down and no longer cares. Like me. There's a strange quietness between us. I look at my wrapper, put the treat in my mouth, and read aloud, *Ignore the clock*.

As if on command, we both look toward the mantel. It's 1:35 in the morning. Instead of doing what the paper suggests, my reticent friend silently rises from the couch. We both know tomorrow is a workday, and we're the types who feel our jobs are how we thrive and survive, especially during a crisis. She retrieves her laptop from the dining room table and stashes it in her briefcase. She slips on her shoes, quietly thanks me for the wine, and heads to the front door. Minimal words are spoken. What can we say to each other after all that has been said and unsaid this evening?

After a hug and her making a weak comment about my pathetic socks, we exchange goodbyes. I thank her sincerely for her help with finances and ask if she is okay walking alone this late at night to her two-bedroom townhouse three buildings over. With masked stubbornness in her voice, she says she's fine and makes her exit.

Behind her, I set the deadbolt since I now know I'm the only one remaining inside.

Something happened with Zoey. I've never seen her this introspective. I can tell you she usually is vibrant and vivacious, but she wasn't tonight. I doubt you notice the difference in her, but I saw her real self for the first time.

After pouring the last few ounces of wine into my glass, I finish them off. Without care or concern, I set the now-empty wine bottles and glasses on the kitchen counter, have the refrigerator Alexa set the alarm and turn off the lights, and head upstairs.

Untaken? Surely, I'm not that, too.

If you're still here, does that mean you're untaken, too?

And if so, what can or will we do about it?

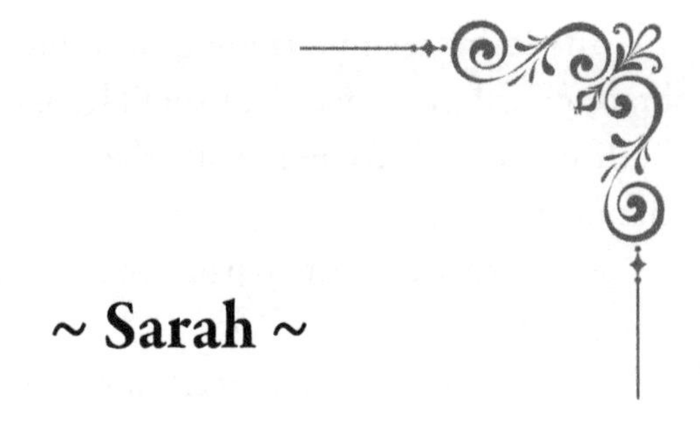

~ Sarah ~

I drag myself up the staircase, knowing I've had way too much to drink. Each step is laborious; my thoughts are fuzzy from mixing Motrin, Ativan, and far too many glasses of wine. I stop on the turned landing at the stair's midpoint to catch my breath; my legs feel weighted down, as though they're encased in cement pavers.

As I near the top stair, the sock's pinky toe's fabric on my left foot—yes, the one with the Y on it—catches on the edge of the stair, causing me to trip. When the slippery sock hits the next step, both legs buckle under my body weight, making my jaw bang against the top stair.

My right foot tries to stop the fall two stairs down, but I slip and slide further.

Down.

In seconds, I try to reach up and grasp the banister rail. My hand misses and becomes entangled between two spindles. There's an audible snap of my wrist.

Down. Slow-motion, down.

Somehow my head is at an awkward angle; I view my kneecap in a strange position as I fall three more stairs.

Down.

The staircase's mid-landing turn interrupts my descent. I brace myself as my face and shoulder slam into the wall and both of my feet connect with the banister's metal spindles simultaneously.

An excruciating, sharp pain seizes my hip and back.

Down.

I tumble in a half somersault down the remaining stairs to the bottom of the staircase.

My fall comes to a halt with a sickening thud when I land on the floor. I lie twisted like a pretzel.

I'm still.

Stuck stiff in my spot.

I'm down.

Immediately, I tell myself to get up, but I realize none of my body parts will obey my commands. I contemplate ways to rescue myself from this predicament, such as calling out for help or using my smartphone. Unfortunately, the phone is still upstairs in its charger.

As I think about other possibilities, darkness envelopes my world, and I pass out.

I DON'T KNOW HOW LONG I've been unconscious.

I try moving but can't.

I try stretching my hands open and can't. My toes refuse to move. Hmm, I can't feel my toes.

I realize I can't feel any part of my body.

Odd. I don't feel any pain. The sharp pain that seemed seconds ago yet an eternity has vanished.

As you can see, one of my eyelids is out of commission, so I try the other one further. Through its slit, I make out the moon's shadow from the second-floor skylight on the wall. I sense a dull green light coming from behind me, which must be from the microwave clock in the kitchen. We still have electricity; it's not another rolling blackout across the city. That must mean the electrical grid was not attacked and no electromagnetic pulse was detonated in the atmosphere.

Has it been minutes or an hour or several days?

I attempt to speak out—I want to call out to Alexa to get someone to come, but I remember her demise when I threw her against the fireplace wall. With false determination, I try to pronounce her name, but can't speak loud enough to awaken the units in the bedrooms or office; I can't go to the kitchen and press the access button on the fridge to alert anyone.

Are you there? Can you help me? Please come and tell me I'm okay. Please help me get up. Can you call for an ambulance or something, someone? Could you call Denny for me? Maybe he's in bed, and you'll have to wake him up.

I force my slitted eye to open more and can only see the bottom of an ugly sock directly in front of me; no happy letters are visible. Strangely enough, I've never seen my foot from this angle. In my stupor, the sock's weird colors taunt me; the individual appendages appear to be waving at me as if pointing to the havoc the pinky toe caused. I want to yell an obscenity at the torturous toe, but words don't form in my mouth. I try to look at the sides of the sock but can't focus. The view is fuzzy and reddish looking. I can't see farther away than my awkward foot.

I still feel no pain, nothing.

I concentrate on how I got here. I recall drinking with Zoey. I go further back in my memory: sleeping, silly socks, taking Motrin and Ativan. Being in Dennis's office. Right, I remember it now. Denny is gone—he left me here alone.

I curse under my breath at the man, my husband.

Ah, yes. I'm alone.

I don't feel in control. In fact, I feel out of control, because I'm lying here in the dark in a perilous position, and I can't move or feel anything.

I have no control.

Can you call Zoey for me? My parents or sister? Or Jeremy? Maybe he's already on his way over here. He's never been to our place before, but I'm sure he can figure out where we live.

After closing my one working eye for several seconds and opening it again, I home in on my hand. Do you notice that it's a grayish color of blue? A blue as if it were dead, and no blood is in it. Maybe the lack of lighting is making it look surreal.

I THINK I PASSED OUT and woke up again. Several times.

THIS TIME, THERE'S a faint but annoying beeping sound that toys with me—I recognize it's Alexa's daily alarm in our bedroom telling us to get up. It must be past dawn, but I can't seem to open either of my eyes.

If it's morning, almost twelve hours have passed since this whole mess started with those two girls on the swings and that odd sound. How long have I been stuck in this position?

An inner darkness envelops me again.

BACK AND FORTH I FLOW from consciousness to unconsciousness; my brain processes events and scenes throughout my life: playing with my sister, Dad tickling me on the living room floor, Mom helping me with a school project, Denny playfully kissing my ear, and so on, memory after memory. Oh, how I love Denny. I love his smile, the way he laughs, and his silly jokes. Memories float by of Mark and Melissa at a company barbecue. Laughing at a bar with Zoey and a temporary boyfriend. Hundreds of memories quickly come and go through my confused brain.

The flashes start taking a turn to the negative: me stealing a piece of candy at the food store at age eight, lying to my parents to get Silvia in trouble, cheating on a college test by copying Rochelle's paper, fantasizing about having sex with the cute guy at the grocery store, plotting schemes of mean things I can do to coworkers to get ahead, my hatred toward Aunt Amy. Oh yes, not wanting to be pregnant, wanting an abortion. And Jeremy—do I dare go there?

Dark secrets and thoughts. Evil things you don't know about me. Things I would never tell anyone, ever. Secrets. Bad thoughts and intentions.

I don't know. I'm so confused.

Where is this all leading me?

I try to move again but can't.

I try to see or hear but no longer can.

I try to move my tongue; I only feel an unbelievable dryness and stiffness. I want to speak, but there's no creation of words, no sounds produced.

Are you still here with me? Can you help me, please?

I feel a rush—a rush of blackness. Not the blackness of being in a dark room where there's no window, but an utter darkness and an outer darkness.

Darkness where I can't tell whether my eyes are open or shut, whether I'm alive or dead.

I start to panic. I try to take a deep breath but can't fill my lungs with air.

Am I dying? Am I dead? Am I to ever have control again?

The blackness is even blacker—if that's possible.

There's an emptiness in the air around me. A chasm I can't explain. The lack of noise makes me more confused and frightened.

I'm scared.

Lonely.

Unfathomable, unutterable loneliness.

I could call out your name, but for some strange reason, I have this abnormal sensation that you're no longer here. Where did you go? Did you abandon me, too, and go to someone else, leaving me all by myself?

No one is nearby. I feel no life around me.

Where am I?

I sense I'm at the edge of a dark abyss and starting to fall into it. I feel empty; I feel cold and hot, supremely uncomfortable. Hungry, yet not knowing what would satisfy me. Everything is at extremes, simultaneously—I've never felt like this before!

Right before I pass out again, I think of Denny. I love you, Den. I'm sorry.

I MAY BE CONSCIOUS again but am unsure. All senses seem to have vanished—no feeling, smelling, seeing, hearing, tasting, or being—yet at the same time, powerful whirlwinds of physical, mental, and spiritual anguish encompass my entire being. Terrible. Unimaginable. Disgusting. Overwhelmingly frightening. Relentless.

No, I feel—something is wrong!

I shouldn't be here.

Am I? Am I in ...?

~ You ~

Hell will be an evil, dark, lonely place.
A place no one wants to be.
I'll say it again but in future tense: "What will you do?"

I POWER DOWN MY KINDLE and set it on the empty airplane seat beside me. I reach up and click off the solo light in the bulkhead above.

Well, that novel was certainly interesting. I'm glad my brother gave me an e-reader for my birthday, and it was great to see him this weekend, but I'm still irked that he uploaded this particular book on it. A book I promised him that I would read.

Adjusting the pillow behind my back, I investigate the darkness outside the airplane window, thirty thousand feet above somewhere in Kansas.

I detest these red-eye flights back to New York. Gives me too much time to think.

My brother's last words to me in San Francisco were "Read the book; it only takes a few hours. It's important. I love you lots."

The book was readable and kept me engaged. But the ending was too depressing. I hate books that end with no finality. Did Sarah live or die? If she lived, was she paralyzed for life? Did her parents or Silvia try contacting her? Did that Jeremy guy or Zoey come to her aid and rescue her? Or did she die and go to Hell? Did Denny and all those people suddenly appear again? Why couldn't the author write that it was all a dream?

Then there's a nagging thought lingering in my brain: the "you" in the book.

Every time Sarah mentions "you," I felt as if she was talking to me, that I was right there with her, trying to help her sort things out and figure out what was happening around her. I felt like I had become a part of her, that I was the person accessing her brain via artificial intelligence. That I was *inside* her head.

Most disturbingly, it caught my attention those times she asked, "What would you do?" or the last time, "What will you do?"

I don't know.

I have no clue what I would do.

I'm not like Sarah, one who hates God or her aunt-in-law or has issues with her husband and a guy potentially pining after her. I am different than her—I go through life not expecting a lot, and I manage those minor bumps in the road with little fanfare or drama.

However, I'm similar to Sarah in that I want to be in control. Doesn't everyone, to some degree? I may not be exactly like her, but I can relate to her wanting life to go her way. Isn't that a form of control? Don't we all want to get what we desire? What we think we need and deserve?

Also, I don't have any personal relationship with God or Jesus. Sure, I've heard Bible verses mentioned throughout my life, but I've largely taken no notice of them, never concentrating on what they might mean.

But what if—what if this Rapture thing were to happen right now while I'm on this airplane zipping across the country? What if the pilot disappears? What if I crash and die this minute? What will happen to me? Where will I go?

I gaze down at my empty hands folded in my lap. I have forgotten everything I have learned in Sunday school, the Bible stories in the Old Testament, and the most important story of how Jesus came to earth and became human, died on the cross, and rose on the third day. I've ignored them through the years. Pushed them off. The "I have no time for God now" approach to life.

Like Sarah, I admit I, too, have a sense of emptiness. I think I have all the answers and go merrily along in life, yet I know inside I'm missing something important. Something transcendent. I feel like that right now. Deep inside, deep in my core. I turn it off over and over, yet it's still there, pleading to get my attention.

Ah, I've been unsure about what I want in this world; I never thought to listen to anything beyond these mortal feelings.

Yes, I want to do everything by myself and believe only in myself.

I go on day by day, planning, scheming, and organizing.

Only to accomplish what?

Nothing.

Sure, I have goals, but what good are they if there's no endgame?

No hereafter, no reason to be alive. Nothing.

There must be a God. Why would I be here? Is death the end of it?

If so, it makes life seem utterly meaningless.

Back to this novel. Was the "you" Sarah kept talking to meant to be me, or was it you, the reader holding this book now?

Or was the "You" someone else?

Could it be, You, God?

Is it You who I need?

Are You trying to get my attention?

Tears form in my eyes as I stare blankly at the back of the airline seat in front of me. I want to get out of my chair and move around, to escape, but I feel frozen in place. Something, Someone, is tugging inside me, at my heart, at the nucleus of my being.

Yes, I'm a sinful person. No one is perfect, not one person. Sinful thoughts, self-centered plans, a corrupted mindset. But I know deep inside that God is an eternal, loving God who can forgive me for everything I've done wrong. Everything.

For some reason, I start to cry.

God, I'm sorry, I'm sorry I've ignored You all these years. I regret that I'm the one who thinks I'm in control. Please forgive me for my past, for my sins, for my selfishness. Only by Your grace and love can You cleanse me. Please come into my life and take over. Show me what You want to do with my life. Please, God, please take control of me.

I believe You died on the cross and shed Your blood many years ago, wiping out all my sins, every sin. You did it in my place, instead of me. And You rose again the third day. You did it for me. I don't want to be untaken if the Rapture occurs right now. Thank You, God, thank You!

As I look up, tears of joy are now streaming down my face.

I no longer feel like those who weren't taken in the story. God is now within me. He loves me, unconditionally! I didn't have to do anything but believe in Him.

I honestly feel an inner peace—I feel rejuvenated, washed clean, whole. I feel God's presence. It's an ineffable peace!

This is what I want. This is what I need!

My brother was reading the Bible to me this morning, and it said:

> *For if we believe that Jesus died and rose again ... Then we which are alive and remain shall be caught up together with them in the clouds, to meet the Lord in the air; and so shall we ever be with the Lord.*

This is what he was talking about—this novel is about the same thing. I remember he said the Bible uses the words "caught up" in the original Greek meaning "to seize, catch (away) up, pluck, pull, take (by force)." Some call it the Rapture today. Some believe it'll happen before the Great Tribulation, when Jesus comes to earth to deal with Satan and those who don't believe in Him.

He said the Tribulation is the world's final seven years of God's curses, punishments, and outpourings of His wrath. It'll be unbelievable and frightening beyond our imaginations:

earthquakes, famine, diseases, objects falling from the sky, death—how can that be? My brother said it's all in the Bible for us to read.

But he said there's an escape from this future event—if you believe in Christ, that He died for your sins on the cross and rose again, you'll live eternally with Him. You'll be taken up to Heaven with others who believe and be saved forever. It's not about your works, what you try to do, but what Jesus has done on the cross for you.

I'd rather choose eternity with Him than outer darkness and pain forever, eternal life rather than eternal death.

For so long I've rejected His offer. Thinking I can do it alone. Thinking I don't need God. Thinking I'm in control.

But now I'm a changed person!

I get it now! I've finally found the peace I've been searching for all these years.

Here's the point: You and I are not in control. You and I are never in control. And you and I never want to be in control, either.

God is the One in control. Of everything.

Yes, I'm not untaken. God loves me unfathomably and unequivocally. Now I am fully assured that I'll be taken in the Rapture.

~ Me ~

The tale is over but I, the writer, have a few words to include.

I didn't want a perfect Christian happily-ever-after story or a typical ending where I cop out by making the tale a dream. And yes, I could do a sequel or two by having someone rescue a paralyzed Sarah, providing perspectives from others of what happens next or during the Tribulation.

As far as Sarah is concerned in this book, it's depressing, but I tried to think like a controlling, self-assured non-believer of Christ. I'm sorry, and I apologize if you're disappointed or don't care for an alpha female character who could easily get on your nerves or reminds you of yourself, which we all do in some ways, especially if we like to be always in control.

Back to "you," the reader: What if you could go inside someone's head and witness everything from only that person's perspective, even if you didn't agree with him or her? Even if you didn't like the individual?

What would you do if you were experiencing such a nightmare through them?

What would you do if the actual Rapture happened today, this minute, this second? Would you be left behind to figure it out?

How would you react to having a friend or family member missing suddenly? Or would you be one of the taken?

Better yet, will you be taken in the air with me to see our Lord if we're alive when it happens? Can you comprehend or believe such a happening? I can't, yet this is my poor attempt at trying to figure out how it may or could happen.

I must confess this story threw me for a loop. Like Sarah, I want to be the one in control and on top of every situation. And like Amy, I'm stubborn about preaching my beliefs in God, not allowing the Holy Spirit to work in those around me. I must remember to "speak the truth in love," but I so often fall short when dealing with others.

God is at work in you and me this second. He's having you read this for a purpose, His purpose.

Think about this: Did someone give you this book to read because they have a burden for you, for your life after death—because they love you but can't explain it or have built up walls between you two? A friend, a family member, or a loved one? Did you get it as a gift and kept putting off reading it until this precise moment? Or did you pick it up on your own, curious to know what the Rapture is, or wanting to learn more about what the Bible tells us about it?

Or it's like this: Every time God, Heaven, and Hell are mentioned in the same sentence, you and the person who gave you this book argue and become more distant from each other. I know—I'm part of the same problem. People like me mean well, truly we do, but we can't present the truth the way God wants us to. We jump the gun and say something at the wrong time.

Please don't lash out at the messenger, but pay attention to the message, however clumsily it's been delivered.

Thank goodness for the Holy Spirit, who intercedes and will prompt or pester you to get you to stop, listen, and believe in Him.

Or maybe you already are a believer who's captivated, like I am, by the idea of a Pre-Tribulation Rapture happening soon. This book was exciting to research and analyze the different interpretations. There may be Biblical errors in it, and things, of course, may not happen the way I imagine. That's why none of it, including the people, is real; it's merely my idea of what it could be like if it took place when I wrote the novel. I could be completely off-base with the scenarios. I'll be the first to admit my faults. But seriously, what if it happened right now?

Is your vision of the Rapture different?

Do you ever think about it and hope for its coming?

Writing this story several times over three decades taught me quite a bit about different theories on the topic. The Bible states that no one knows when the Rapture will occur. Some believe it will be before the Tribulation, yet others think it will begin after the Tribulation has started or in the middle or end of the seven years. God is a loving God with perfect timing in all things, so He will rescue His people at the right time. My belief (and hope) is that it will happen at the beginning, as I selfishly do not want to live through the intense destruction.

Scripture says both the dead and alive in Christ will be caught up. What a fantastic concept. If the Rapture doesn't happen in our time, while we're on this earth, we who believe in Him and die have the assurance that we will be raised with those alive when it does happen. Better yet, if we've already left these earthly bodies behind, we will precede those who are alive in Christ when He calls for us.

My research also led me to believe that the Lord's shout, archangel's voice, and the trump of God mentioned in 1 Thessalonians 4:16 will possibly be heard by both believers and unbelievers. I base this on the Apostle Paul's Damascus conversion when those with him heard Christ speaking to Paul but couldn't understand or see Him. I don't think an unbeliever will be able to decipher the shout or conceive what is happening at that moment. But I do think he or she may hear something—like an indiscernible sound, which could be explained away as the "cause" of the missing loved ones.

Another phenomenon that may be thoroughly confusing is the question of children. Since the New Testament never mentions children during the Tribulation except for references to those who are with child or nursing (meaning pregnancies or those born during the seven years), one could speculate that all the rest of the children already have been taken to Heaven in the Rapture. Some theologians have considered that there could be an age of accountability for a child to believe in Christ—an age when a young person decides to turn his or her life over to God. If so, what age would it be? The age of ten to twelve came up often in my research, but only the Lord knows our hearts, including a child's. He knows all His children personally.

There's the discussion about the unborn. My only thought was that if a pregnant mother is a believer and is raptured, I doubt the child in her womb would fall out of her onto the floor. So why wouldn't all unborn or newborns be taken, too?

The mentally handicapped may be considered as children and raptured also. I don't know, nor do I have all the answers.

As you know, I have taken the liberty of including these speculations in my story. Please don't hold me accountable; I'm only mentioning these things to get you, the reader, to think more deeply about the topic.

Lastly, I could come to no conclusions in researching the issue of a second chance. If you hear the Word of God and don't believe, and the Rapture happens, will you get a second chance? Will you be able to change your mind during the Tribulation? There will be those saved during those days, but were they given the eternal plan of salvation before the Rapture occurred and rejected it?

A Bible verse that could be applied is 2 Thessalonians 2:10–12:

> *... because they received not the love of the truth, that they might be saved. And for this cause God shall send them strong delusion, that they should believe a lie; That they all might be damned who believed not the truth, but had pleasure in unrighteousness.*

I don't know at what point the Holy Spirit determines or relinquishes His love toward you if you're not a believer but have heard the plan of salvation. I don't know when God, who knows exactly who will become believers, turns His back on those who refuse to believe.

This is the scariest part of contemplating the event of the Rapture itself. The Bible clearly states that a delusion will befall those who are untaken. I would hate for you to fall into that trap, a trap leading to eternal damnation.

What if you're like Sarah and refuse God?

What if you only get one chance and the Rapture happens?

What if you turn your back on God?

What if you think you're in control?

Wouldn't that make you concerned enough to make sure you're a follower of Christ for eternity?

I don't know where you are in your relationship with God. If you think you're not good or worthy enough to be one of His children, please don't. Everyone is no good, including me as a believer. Only Jesus can save us—not through our works and the things we do, but because of His endless love, grace, and mercy when He shed His blood on the cross for our sins and died for us. Our faith in Him changes us.

If this time, right now as you read these words, the Holy Spirit's prompting you, please listen to Him. He's here for you, always.

Believe in Him now. Reread the prior chapter and prayer with a tender heart and be assured you won't be taken by surprise.

The Rapture may or may not happen today, tomorrow, next week, or years from now, but when it does, I hope and pray to see you there, in the clouds, as we spend forever with the Lord.

The End.

The Eternal Plan of Salvation

taken from *the King James Version of the Bible*

For all have sinned, and come short of the glory of God;
~ Romans 3:23

For the wages of sin is death; but the gift of God is eternal life through Jesus Christ our Lord.
~ Romans 6:23

That if thou shalt confess with thy mouth the Lord Jesus, and shalt believe in thine heart that God hath raised him from the dead, thou shalt be saved. For with the heart man believeth unto righteousness; and with the mouth confession is made unto salvation. For the scripture saith, Whosoever believe on Him shall not be ashamed. For there is no difference between the Jew and the Greek: for the same Lord over all is rich unto all that

call upon Him. For whosoever shall call upon the name of the Lord shall be saved.

~ Romans 10:9-13

But God commendeth his love toward us, in that, while we're yet sinners, Christ died for us.

~ Romans 5:8

Verses Regarding the Rapture

taken from *the King James Version of the Bible*

Behold, I shew you a mystery: We shall not all sleep, but we shall all be changed, In a moment, in the twinkling of an eye, at the last trump: for the trumpet shall sound, and the dead shall be raised incorruptible, and we shall be changed. For this corruptible must put on incorruption, and this mortal must put on immortality.
~ I Corinthians 15:51-53

For the Lord himself shall descend from heaven with a shout, with the voice of the archangel, and with the trump of God: and the dead in Christ shall rise first: Then we which are alive and remain shall be caught up together with them in the clouds, to meet the Lord in the air: and so shall we ever be with the Lord.
~ I THESSALONIANS 4:16-17

Discussion Questions

1. Would you want to be in someone's head and know everything they are thinking, seeing, hearing, and feeling, even if you disagreed with them? If so, why?
2. Do you think a sound of some sort will be heard by those who are unbelievers when the Rapture happens?
3. Do you think all children (including those in the womb) will be taken during the Rapture? What do you think could be the age of accountability?
4. Do you think those who have heard the eternal plan of salvation before the Rapture occurs and reject it will get a second chance to accept Christ during the Tribulation?
5. Whether the Rapture happens today, tomorrow, or years from now, will you be taken or untaken when it occurs?

.

This book was originally titled *Untakenable* and has been updated in 2023.
Cover Photo: Kaleb Kendall / StockSnap
Editor: Angie Peters

If you enjoyed this novel, please help spread the Word by posting positive comments online as it is appreciated.

constanceowyler@gmail.com

About the Author

Born and raised in Southern California, Wyler is a Christian who lives in the Pacific Northwest. Having owned a business for over thirty years, she is retired and enjoys spending time with her family and traveling.

Lightning Source UK Ltd.
Milton Keynes UK
UKHW010751060223
416537UK00008B/2059